Mrs Bennet's Surprising Connections

Prequel to 'Don't flatter yourself'

A P&P spin-off

Sydney Salier

This is a work of fiction. The characters, locations, and events portrayed in this book are fictitious or are used fictitiously. Any similarity to real persons, living or dead is purely coincidental and not intended by the author.

ISBN: 9781704420196

To Michael

Thanks

Sydney Salier

CONTENTS

List of major characters

Amelia Flinter, Duchess of Denton	Mother of Lady Francine
Duke of Denton	Father of Lady Francine
Lady Francine	Daughter of the Duke and Duchess of Denton
James, Earl Fellmar	Husband of Lady Francine
Lady Elizabeth	Daughter of Earl Fellmar and Lady Francine
Mr Thomas Bennet	Master of Longbourn, Meryton, Hertfordshire
Mrs Francine Bennet	Nee Gardiner, wife of Thomas Bennet
Jane Bennet	Daughter of Thomas Bennet
Mr Henry Bennet	Father of Thomas Bennet
Mrs Emma Bennet	Mother of Thomas Bennet
Mrs Anne Hopkins	Companion to the Duchess of Denton
Alexander, Marquess Denmere	Brother to Lady Francine
Lady Penelope	Alexander's wife
Alistair Flinter	Grandson of the Duchess of Denton
Robert Flinter	Twin brother of Alistair Flinter
Andrew Fitzwilliam, Earl Matlock	Friend of the Duchess of Denton
Lady Catherine	Sister of the Earl Matlock

1 *Meetings at Almack's*

1782

Her Grace, Amelia Flinter, the Duchess of Denton, looked on with amusement at the manoeuvrings going on across the room at Almack's. Her son Alexander, Marquess Denmere, appeared to be the focal point for many of the young ladies who were vying for his attention.

Even without the bias of a mother's affection, Alexander was a very desirable addition to the marriage mart. The son of the Duke was tall and well built, handsome and charming. The young ladies, and some not so young, were fluttering like butterflies around an exotic bloom. Alexander was thoroughly enjoying himself. At the age of twenty, he had not yet become either blasé or cynical about the attention being showered upon him.

The two most assiduous ladies appeared to be Lady Catherine Fitzwilliam and Lady Penelope Bronsant. Lady Catherine was the younger sister of Earl Matlock, whose excellent reputation and wealth, made his sister eminently eligible.

Lady Penelope, whose father was the Duke of Cardic, was even better positioned. She was also the prettier of the two.

The Duchess, who knew her son well, immediately realised that Alexander was more interested in the softer look of the second girl. She hoped that if it went any further, there would be more to interest him than a pretty face. After all, he would have to spend many years in her company.

She knew only too well how incompatible personalities could make life difficult in a marriage. Even though she had never been romantic, she had expected at least to become friends with her husband. Instead, they were still virtual strangers after one and twenty years of marriage. He was always polite to her but had no interest in her ideas or her opinions.

It had started so well. Considering that her parents were the Duke and Duchess of Brastone, she learned from an early age that she would be expected to marry for duty. To her, at the time, it seemed a good reason. That was what one did.

She had her coming out when she was sixteen and in her first season had met the young Duke of Denton, who at the age of five and twenty had seemed very mature and exceedingly charming. She had been flattered when he paid attention to her. Her parents had been overjoyed. He was then of prime marriageable age, and everyone expected him to select a wife in short order. While he courted her, he appeared to listen to her every opinion. Therefore, when he offered for her, she was most happy to accept.

In retrospect, she suspected that her husband had chosen her only for her connection and dowry.

After they were married, she found out that he had listened so attentively, because he had very little conversation himself. Apart from politics, a subject which in his opinion was incomprehensible to the female mind, and therefore not worth the bother to discuss with his wife, he was only interested in sport. Whereas sport was a subject, Amelia truly had no interest in, although like any good wife of her acquaintance, she had perfected the art of appearing to listen while her mind was elsewhere.

Therefore, apart from ensuring that they had the requisite, heir and a spare, as well as an accidental late-arriving daughter, they rarely saw each other. He spent most of his time in London, particularly when parliament was sitting, while she stayed predominantly at their estate. Although she did not ask, and he was very discreet, she was certain that a major attraction of London was his mistress. As long as he was discreet and did not embarrass her, she did not care.

Since she and her husband spent little time in each other's company, she had devoted her life to look after their tenants, her children, and her friends.

She was also an inveterate matchmaker. Unlike most of the match-making mothers, though, she was interested in matching people who had a chance to be happy together.

Although she usually looked for matches of similar status, she had no problems with people of good character, who were technically of a lower station, as long as the personalities were compatible.

She sometimes wondered if she had turned into a romantic after all. Then she decided that it only made sense to marry somebody with whom you could be comfortable. That was only logical.

And now she watched the literal and figurative dance going on between her older son and the ladies.

She was so engrossed in the view that she did not notice the gentleman approach. 'Your Grace, what a delight to see you again.'

Startled out of her reverie, the Duchess looked at the speaker and gave him a genuine smile. 'Lord Matlock, how wonderful to see you as well. It has been much too long,' she addressed her old friend.

'It has indeed. I gather we are here for similar reasons?' Andrew Fitzwilliam, the Earl of Matlock looked at the group surrounding Alexander, which included his much younger sister, Lady Catherine.

'It was a pity your father died at the beginning of the last season. Your sister must have been devastated on at least two accounts,' Amelia Flinter was sympathetic to her old friend.

'She was undeniably upset. Perhaps that is why she is trying to make up for lost time this season. I have hardly seen my bed because of the number of balls to which I had to escort her.'

'How is your wife? I hear congratulations are in order again,' the duchess smiled.

'She is as well as can be expected. Richard, on the other hand, is doing extremely well. He has a powerful set of lungs and can make himself heard in the whole house,' the proud father boasted ever so slightly.

The duchess laughed. 'In that case, he might be destined for a military career. He will be able to make himself heard even on a battlefield.'

'Heaven forfend. Susan would worry herself sick,' protested Fitzwilliam.

'I also hear that your sister Anne has become engaged to George Darcy.'

'Indeed, she has. Those two are besotted with each other. I am delighted about it though. Particularly since Pemberley is not too far from Matlock, Anne and Susan will be able to visit quite easily when we are at home,' Lord Matlock declared. 'But enough of me, how is your family. I can see that Alexander is well, but what about the others?'

'Francine is a joy. At the age of ten, she is already becoming quite the lady,' the Duchess smiled fondly, thinking about her young daughter. 'Robert, on the other hand, is becoming more reckless by the day. I worry that one day he will break his neck, racing his horses. But since my husband encourages him, there is nothing I can say.'

Fitzwilliam laughed. 'I am sorry, Your Grace, but I remember a very young hoyden who challenged me to a race. Do you remember her perchance?' he finished with a twinkle in his eyes.

'Yes, I do remember her, but she grew out of that phase by the time she was Robert's age,' disclaimed Amelia.

'Far be it from me to cast aspersions on your veracity, but I believe one can never out-grow such a basic trait of character. At best one can camouflage it successfully,' he smiled at her.

With twinkling eyes, she conceded, 'perhaps.'

The Earl of Matlock changed the subject. 'What think you of a match between Alexander and Catherine?'

'Much as I like you, I do not think those two are suited,' replied the Duchess.

'More's the pity. I would have liked to count you as family. But even I can see where his interest lies,' conceded the Earl.

'It is early days yet. We have to wait and see.'

~~MrsB~~

Meanwhile, Lady Catherine was fuming. She was determined to make the most advantageous match possible. As the daughter and sister to an Earl, she had excellent connections, only marginally inferior to Lady Penelope, whose father, although a Duke, was very retiring and therefore had not much influence in the House of Lords. She herself had much better connections.

And yet, Marquess Denmere paid attention to Lady Penelope rather than herself. What did that girl have, other than a pretty face?

Although Lady Catherine would not admit this even to herself, she was angry with her father for dying at such an inconvenient time, robbing her of the previous season. She had been so very excited to be presented and then attending her first ball on the day of her eighteenth birthday. She had looked forward to meeting charming and attentive gentlemen and having her pick of potential husbands. She knew she was not the prettiest woman, but she was striking in appearance.

Then, not a week later, her hopes were dashed. Her father died, and although they had not been overly close, society expected her to mourn him. By the time she was allowed to re-join society, the season was over.

Now she was resolved to make up for missed opportunities. Marquess Denmere was everything she wanted in a husband, good looking, amiable, an excellent dancer and, most importantly, the oldest son of a Duke. She would have him, and Lady Penelope would have to look elsewhere.

~~MrsB~~

Lady Penelope hovered at the edge of the group surrounding the Marquess Denmere. She was a shy young lady and had only recently come out into society and was still uncomfortable in large gatherings. Staying in the group around the Marquess felt relatively safe.

He made a point of including her in the conversation. Admittedly, he was titled and handsome, but she felt he was gentle. She did not even realise that she was smiling at the young man more than she usually did. She only knew that she would dearly get to know him better and maybe have a friend in such gatherings.

After all, with all those ladies competing for his attention, he could not possibly be interested in a shy wallflower, as she thought of herself. But it was marvellous when he smiled at her.

~~MrsB~~

The Marquess was a gregarious young man by nature. He was having a delightful time chatting with all those lovely young ladies.

He was, of course, aware that he was on the marriage mart, but he was not in any hurry to choose a bride. He was at Almack's because it was expected of him. But that did not stop him from enjoying the company.

He was amused at Lady Catherine's attention, rightly considering her to be a woman who was more interested in status than marital felicity. Although he expected to marry someone of similar consequence, like his mother, he hoped to find someone with whom he could at least be friends.

Lady Catherine did not measure up to his ideas. On the other hand, there was this obviously shy young woman who appeared to be very sweet. He delighted in drawing her into the conversation and was pleased when he received a grateful smile for his efforts. He hoped she would be at many of the events he expected to attend.

~~MrsB~~

2 *Actions & Consequences*

1782

Dinner at Denton House, the following week, was a very successful affair. The guests included the Duke and Duchess of Cardic and their daughter, Lady Penelope, the Earl of Matlock and his sister, Lady Catherine Fitzwilliam. Young Baron Standby rounded out the numbers.

Soon after dark, young Barton, the butler's son came to inform the Duke that it had started to snow heavily. Convinced that the snow would stop in short order, the Duke encouraged his guests to remain and wait to go home when the weather cleared.

By the time it had gotten so late that the guests needed to leave, so much snow had fallen and was still falling, that it was impossible for most of them the reach their homes.

Under the circumstances, the only thing to do was to offer rooms to spend the night to all the guests. The unexpected guests filled the house to capacity, but nobody had to share a room.

Since there was now no need to concern themselves about braving the cold, the gentlemen soon congregated in the library and the billiards room, where several of them made severe inroads into the supply of port and brandy. Eventually, even the most hardened drinkers retired to their rooms. One of the last to bed was Alexander, who was rather under the weather. He definitely needed the assistance of his valet and was asleep as soon as his head touched the pillow.

~~MrsB~~

As it happened to her occasionally, particularly after an evening of entertaining when her mind refused to settle, the Duchess left her rooms to collect some reading material from the library. Since she was very familiar with the house, she did not trouble taking a light as the occasional lamp was sufficient for her to see, and very quietly, she ghosted through the hallways.

As she rounded a corner to pass her son's bedroom, she spied another form in the hall, quietly opening the door to Alexander's room. Even in the dim light, she could discern that the form was obviously female and clad in nightclothes, which in this case had been supplied by the hostess. Based on her observation of dark hair and quite a tall frame, she had more than a suspicion about the identity of the interloper.

'You really do not want to go there, Lady Catherine,' the Duchess said in a low voice, startling the lady so addressed.

'Mind your own business,' Lady Catherine snapped, assuming the voice belonged to a maid.

The Duchess was more amused than offended, although poor manners were abhorrent to her. 'My son is my business, and since you are obviously trying to compromise him, your behaviour is my business too.'

'He invited me, Your Grace,' Lady Catherine blustered.

'My dear girl, even if he was sober enough to invite you, which I doubt, it was your duty to decline the invitation. Otherwise, you will be considered to be a harlot.'

'He compromised me; he will simply have to marry me,' Catherine protested.

The Duchess was shaking her head. 'You just compromised yourself by being where you have no right to be. I am sorry, my dear, but as much as I like your brother, I prefer my son to marry a woman who will not embarrass him. For your brother's sake, I will forget what I saw today. Do we understand each other?'

When Catherine did not respond, the Duchess continued quietly, 'you had best go back to your room and give up this scheme of yours. Because of tonight, you will never succeed. If you try again, I will speak out against you, and *no* man will want to marry you. Do you understand?'

'You would ruin me?' Lady Catherine was shocked.

'No, you ruined yourself by your actions tonight, and you need to learn that actions have consequences,' came the merciless reply.

Lady Catherine looked into the implacable eyes of the Duchess and conceded defeat. 'I seem to have lost my way in the dark. Thank you for pointing me in the right direction. Goodnight, Your Grace.'

'Goodnight, Lady Catherine.'

~~MrsB~~

By morning it had stopped snowing. Servants had been sent to collect clothing for the guests from their homes, but there was still too much snow on the road for carriages to move about safely.

The guests at Denton House settled in for a relaxing day. The men were spending most of their time in the library but joined the ladies for meals and tea.

The young men of the party made the most of the opportunity to chat with the young ladies since it was a rare occurrence to spend so much time in each other's company. Lady Catherine appeared a little subdued but spoke politely to the Baron.

Alexander, Marquess Denmere, was happy to flirt with Lady Penelope. He was intrigued by her shy demeanour and kept trying to draw her out. She found it difficult to speak to him since he had captured her interest, but propriety demanded that she be demure. At the same time, she abhorred the idea of being perceived as coy. As a result, Alexander had to work hard to get her to speak to him.

Lady Penelope, do you enjoy reading?' he asked, hoping to find a topic agreeable to her and was rewarded with a happy smile.

'I take great pleasure in the plays of Mr Shakespeare, Lord Denmere, although I must admit I prefer his comedies. I do so adore stories with a happy ending.' She blushed at venturing her opinion.

'Do you have a favourite?' He was curious to learn more.

'I do so love *A Midsummer Night's Dream*,' Lady Penelope replied, blushing even more. 'I think it quite magical.'

Alexander smiled, and half teasingly replied, 'you would make a wonderful Fairy Queen.'

To which Lady Penelope protested, 'you flatter me unconscionably. I have seen the play at the theatre, and I am not nearly beautiful enough.'

'On the contrary, you do not give yourself nearly enough credit. I think you are very beautiful.'

He delighted in being able to get her to open up a little. Having to make such an effort had an interesting effect on the young man. Since Lady Penelope was not throwing herself at him, he wanted to get to know her better. Much better.

Both Duchesses noticed his interest and exchanged glances which told each of them that the interest was welcome.

Over the next few weeks, they managed to arrange things in such a way that the two young people were often in company. Such proximity eventually resulted in Alexander proposing to Lady Penelope with her parents' approval. The families were of the same rank and similar wealth; therefore, by society's standards, they were a perfect match. That they liked each other was even better as far as their mothers were concerned. As a matter of fact, that liking was *considerably* more on both sides.

In May of that year, Marquess Denmere married Lady Penelope. After their four months-long wedding tour, they settled at Denton Manor to await a joyous event. The young wife had just noticed her condition and shared her news with her excited husband.

~~MrsB~~

3 *Upheaval*

1783

With February, the time of Lady Penelope's confinement arrived. The lady was very happy to have done with this pregnancy, which had been hard on her. She was terrified at the potential size of the baby, but it was too late to change her mind.

Both Duchesses were at her bedside, while Alexander paced the floor in the library. Since parliament was sitting, the Duke of Denton was in London.

Just before dawn the next morning, the Duchess of Denton delivered the news to her son. He was the father of *two* beautiful boys, at which point his face lit up. Unfortunately, the birth had been too much for Lady Penelope, and she had not survived.

Alexander was devastated. He rushed to his wife's room, where her mother and the midwife had cleaned her up, and she lay on the bed as if sleeping.

He was sitting on the bed, holding the hand of his still wife, when the midwife and his mother-in-law carried in his sons.

'Take them away. I have no wish to see them. They killed my beautiful wife,' he snapped at them.

The women were shocked at his response but acceded to his wishes.

He was in mourning for a full year. He was so despondent he barely spoke to anyone. He resolutely refused to see his sons or have anything to do with them.

~~MrsB~~

Eventually, the pain became bearable, but he promised himself, he would never again allow himself to become enamoured of a woman. He would enjoy them, but none would ever again touch his heart.

He moved to London, where he bought his own townhouse. He did not wish to live at Denton House under the eye of his own father. While the Duke lived his own life as he wished, without reference to his wife, he was a stickler for discretion, at least where his children were concerned.

Therefore, Alexander settled into his own townhouse, to lead the kind of life that would let him forget his pain. While he was still a very attractive prospect on the marriage mart, after all, he was a very young, handsome, and titled widower, he had no interest in another wife.

He had his obligatory heir and a spare, whom he avoided as much as possible because they reminded him of his dead wife. While he no longer held them responsible for her death, they were still the cause of it, and it pained him to see them. He never realised the pain he was causing them by his indifference.

While each year he became more debauched, his sons found allies; their beloved grandmother and their aunt, who ensured that the pain from their father's disregard was minimised.

~~MrsB~~

While her son was grieving for his departed wife, life still had to go on at Denton Manor. Therefore, in April, the Duchess was again planning to make her weekly visit to the tenants. Eleven-year-old Francine begged to come along to escape the sombre atmosphere in the house.

'Mama, do you think Alexander was very much in love with his wife?' She enquired of the Duchess. 'Is that why he is so very sad now?'

Her mother gave her a wistful smile. 'Yes, I believe he was and still is. I wish I could ease his sorrow so that he could see what wonderful sons he now has. But in time, he will feel better.'

Francine looked pensive. 'The novels all say it is wonderful to be in love. But he suffers so much. I wondered if I would want to fall in love if it means I will feel such distress.'

'I always felt that you should treasure the good moments and good feelings. They more than make up for the grief you encounter at other times. If you always anticipate the pain, you will never feel the joy.' The Duchess gave Francine an encouraging smile. 'But enough of that now, we have our duties to perform, not spend the whole morning wool-gathering.'

When they exited the house, the groom had their phaeton ready. While the footman helped them board, he said, 'Mrs Carter has packed all the baskets you asked for, and they are stowed in the box behind the seat as usual.'

The Duchess gave him a pleasant nod. 'Thank you, John. And thank the housekeeper for me.'

'Whom are we visiting today, Mama?'

'We are going to the Potter's first. Mrs Carter tells me that Mrs Potter has been sick for a few days already. I had her pack extra food for them since Mrs Potter is too ill to cook and the children still need to eat. There is also some soup and medicines for Mrs Potter. Hopefully, they will improve her soon.'

While they drove across the estate, they chatted about trivial things until they reached the Potter's cottage.

As they approached the open door, they noticed to their surprise that Mrs Potter had a most unusual visitor already. The lady was in the kitchen with her sleeves pushed up, and up to her elbows in soapy water, while admonishing the children to eat their porridge.

The Duchess looked more closely, yes, her first impression of defining the person as a lady was correct, despite the labour she was performing at the moment. Although she wore a mourning dress, it was of good quality, and she moved with grace.

As the oldest girl noticed the latest visitors, she rose from the table and curtsied. 'Good morning, Your Grace, Lady Francine.' She said politely.

The lady at the tub turned around and blushed as she saw whom the girl had greeted. She also curtsied while trying to work out what to do with her wet hands. 'Your Grace, pardon me for not being able to greet you properly.'

'Never mind, I can see that you are busy.' Then the Duchess turned to the young girl who had greeted her. 'Sophie, would you be so good as to introduce us?'

'Your Grace, this is our cousin Anne Hopkins,' the blushing girl said.

Anne Hopkins spoke up. 'I am staying with my family at The Meadows since I recently lost my husband. I came to visit my cousin, Katherine and found everything in quite a state. It appears Mr Potter was reluctant to call for help.'

'We heard via our housekeeper that Mrs Potter was sick and thought we would bring some supplies to see them through until Mrs Potter can look after things again,' explained the Duchess.

'That is very kind of you. My cousin is awake at the moment. Would you like to see her?' Mrs Hopkins offered.

The Duchess accepted the offer, and Mrs Hopkins showed her to the bedroom of Mrs Potter and then withdrew. The lady appeared very weak and a little embarrassed to have such an important visitor.

The Duchess tried to put her at ease. 'You have had us quite worried Mrs Potter. Whyever did you not send word that you needed help?'

'We did not want to be a bother, Your Grace. My husband and I thought we could manage,' Mrs Potter explained. 'And today, Anne arrived. That was a godsend. She is wonderful with the children. It is such a pity that her husband was lost at sea.'

'Her husband was a sailor?' the Duchess questioned.

'No ma'am, he was a Naval Officer,' protested Mrs Potter quite proudly. 'He was such a good man. But now the poor dear will have to find a position to make ends meet. She does not want to be a burden on her family. The Meadows is a good estate, but it cannot support that many people at the moment.'

'Yes, I have heard that they had some problems with the harvests for a couple of seasons,' the Duchess agreed. 'But I had better let you get some rest now. I will visit again next week. In the meantime, just remember if you need assistance, send word. You and your husband are good tenants, and we want you to do and *be* well.'

With that, the Duchess made her good-byes and left the room. She re-entered the kitchen in a thoughtful mood. The kitchen was now much tidier than upon her arrival. The children had finished their porridge and were helping to clean up under the direction of Mrs Hopkins. Even Francine was helping, which brought a smile to the Duchess' face.

When Mrs Hopkins noticed the Duchess, she tentatively offered tea, which the lady gratefully accepted. The children were sent out to perform some small chores and show Francine some puppies, while the adults sat down to their refreshments and conversation.

The Duchess inquired about Anne's background and found her surprisingly well educated and very pleasant company. She appeared to be about thirty or two and thirty years of age, trim and with light brown hair and hazel eyes. Mrs Hopkins told her that she was planning to remain with her cousin until she recovered enough to look after her family again. Remembering Mrs Hopkins' circumstances, the Duchess formed an idea and decided to find out if it was viable. 'What are your plans after your cousin recovers, Mrs Hopkins?'

'I do not yet know what I shall do, other than to look for a position. You see, my husband, who was a Naval Officer, was lost at sea three months ago. Even though we were not blessed with children, the funds available to me are insufficient to live on. He was not in a position to leave me well enough provided to live without earning an income.' This was said without rancour or self-pity.

The Duchess heartily approved of her attitude. 'Would you consider becoming a companion to a somewhat eccentric middle-aged lady?' she asked.

'I suppose that would depend on the eccentricity. As long as the peculiarity is not harmful to anyone, I expect I could accommodate such a lady,' Mrs Hopkins replied thoughtfully.

'The lady I have in mind is rather outspoken, but cannot be so in public, where she must maintain decorum. She also has wide-ranging interests not normally acceptable in ladies and would like a chance to discuss her interests with someone intelligent who will not be offended or censorious,' the Duchess explained with a now somewhat mischievous smile.

'That is the kind of eccentricity I would thoroughly enjoy,' Anne laughed. 'If this lady is authentic and in need of a companion, I would most certainly like an opportunity to meet her.'

'I am delighted you feel this way. You have already met your new employer,' the Duchess smiled broadly.

'You, Your Grace? You want me as your companion?' Anne was shocked and delighted, as she too had found the company over the last half hour very agreeable.

'I gather you are amenable to this idea?' the Duchess smiled.

'I am stunned and delighted to accept your offer, Your Grace. If you are quite certain...'

'I am certain. You will be a breath of fresh air. Now that that is settled, I have two more calls to make and had better be going.' The Duchess became brisk. 'I will send a carriage for you and your things when you are ready to leave here.'

The Duchess gathered Francine, and they went on to make the other planned visits.

Two weeks later, Mrs Anne Hopkins was installed as companion to the Duchess at Denton Manor. Within weeks a firm friendship had formed between her and the Duchess.

The Duchess was grateful for the presence of Anne when at the end of June, she received a letter informing her that her son Robert had died in an accident, while at school in Cambridge. His death devastated the Duchess. She had joked that he would meet his end due to his love of horses and speed, but she had not truly expected it to happen. Several times, late at night, Anne Hopkins was the shoulder for the Duchess to cry on. Eventually, she came to terms with his death, remembering he had died doing something he loved. She missed him, but life went on.

~~MrsB~~

4 *Child's Play*

1784 to 1786

Another year had passed, and since the mourning period for Alexander was over, he had removed to London. He now avoided Denton Manor as much as possible.

The Duke also was in London again, ostensibly for the sitting of parliament.

Although the Duchess inwardly still mourned her son, outwardly she was much as ever.

The Duchess, Lady Francine and Anne Hopkins enjoyed the peace at Denton Manor. Or at least as much peace as two eighteen-month-old rascals would allow. They kept their nurses fully occupied chasing after them. Francine quipped that they would be explorers when they grew up because they were already exploring *everything*. Unless the nurses were exceedingly vigilant, one or both boys managed to escape the nursery on a regular basis. Now that they could even run after a fashion, they appeared unstoppable.

More and more frequently, the ladies took pity on the nurses and took the boys out into the garden to play. Each of them insisted that this was purely for the benefit of the nurses. After all, what lady would find pleasure in the incomprehensible chattering of eighteen-month-old boys, even if they had the most charming smiles. And of course, it could never be, that the hilarity they enjoyed, could have been caused by the antics of either of the twins.

This particular day, while they were entertaining and being entertained by the boys on the lawn beside the house, they noticed a rider ambling up the drive.

When he realised, he had been seen, he dismounted and walked over to them, leading his horse. He lifted his hat and bowed. 'Pardon me ladies for intruding upon you, but I suspect I have lost my way. My friend, Richard Cartwright, invited me to visit and gave me directions as to find him. I am certain my coachman would have no trouble finding his estate. But I chose to ride in this beautiful weather and was admiring the lovely scenery hereabouts; therefore, I believe I was not paying enough attention to the road. Pray tell me this is Bridgeview House. Although since I cannot see a bridge, I conjecture you will inform me that I am wrong.'

The Duchess smiled sweetly to disguise the fact that she was trying very hard not to laugh. 'You are correct, sir, in your assumption that you are wrong. This is Denton Manor. Bridgeview House is two miles back along the road.'

'You are most kind in your correction, but I just realised I have been abominably rude not to have introduced myself. It completely slipped my mind, since usually there is somebody around to do the honours. But I ramble on again. I am David Bryant, of Impington in Cambridgeshire. May I have the pleasure of knowing whom I have been addressing so impudently?' he smiled charmingly.

The Duchess laughed. 'I was wondering how long it would take for you to remember your manners. I am the Duchess of Denton, and these are my daughter Lady Francine and my companion Mrs Hopkins.'

Mr Bryant looked remorseful. 'Dear me, now I am doubly mortified that I have intruded upon you. But I am also beyond delighted to have made the acquaintance of such beautiful and charming ladies.' He now gave them a brilliant smile.

'You sir, are a flatterer,' laughed the Duchess.

'No, Your Grace. Although it pains me, I must disagree with you.' He looked mock offended; then he continued with a twinkle in his eyes. 'You are all charm and graciousness personified. Therefore, I was speaking the literal truth. But now I must not intrude any longer. I have trespassed on your indulgence for too long already. I bid you adieu and hope that I may have the great pleasure of your company again under more fitting circumstances.' He again lifted his hat and bowed, then turned around to mount his horse.

He was delayed in his action when he found a toddler hugging the front leg of his stallion, while the same stallion whiffled the giggling boy's hair.

'Oh dear. Who have we here? I am sorry young man, but your new friend has to leave now.' With those words, Mr Bryant gently picked up the boy and turning, handed him to Mrs Hopkins, who had approached to rescue the stallion from Robert's enthusiasm.

'I am sorry, sir, Robert is overly fond of horses,' she explained.

'He is well matched with Hermes then. He adores children. We sometimes wonder if he thinks he was supposed to be a pony,' chuckled Mr Bryant. Making a show of looking around for any further impediments to his departure, he gave a final bow and mounted. 'Farewell, until another time.'

He directed Hermes to carefully walk back to the driveway, where he turned back a final time and gave a wave before setting the stallion to a trot.

The Duchess muttered in appreciation, 'he has a nice seat.'

~~MrsB~~

The following week an invitation to tea arrived from Richard Cartwright's aunt.

Since there were no girls Francine's age in the Cartwright household, only the Duchess and Mrs Hopkins attended.

Mrs Cartwright was a pleasant lady of middle age with greying hair. She was rake-thin and no beauty, but she had a lively and mischievous smile. Her husband had died two years previously, and she had recently come to live with Mr Cartwright, to act as his hostess. On this day, her nephew and his guest joined her for tea.

For a while, the group discussed the usual polite subjects. But then they digressed.

The Duchess asked Mr Cartwright, 'have you and Mr Bryant been friends for a long time?'

'We met at Cambridge about fifteen years ago. Our fathers had been friends when they were students. They both were enthusiastic chess players, and after university, they played many games by correspondence.

Then, when I was in my second year, my father asked me to look out for Bryant, who was just starting,' Cartwright explained.

'Getting me into trouble, more likely,' interjected Bryant.

Cartwright laughed. 'That is debatable. Whose idea was it, to raid the strawberries in the Dean's garden?'

Bryant waved his hands in a dismissive manner. 'How was I to know that he was planning to have them served at that function. But I heard several people commenting, how much they enjoyed the cherry trifle.' He turned to the ladies. 'Do you also love strawberries?'

'I must confess, I love fresh picked strawberries. But by the time they get to London, they seem to lose their flavour,' the Duchess replied. 'Which is part of the reason why I like to spend the summer at the estate.

'What about you, Mrs Hopkins. Can you resist strawberries?' Bryant asked.

'I like them, but for me, a crisp, tart apple tastes like heaven,' admitted Anne.

Mrs Cartwright smiled. 'Personally, I prefer cherries.' Then she turned to the Duchess. 'I hear you have two delightful grandsons.'

'It is questionable whether I would apply the word delightful to them. But, although I admit to a bias, they are charming rascals. Lively, curious and always getting into mischief,' laughed the Duchess.

For the next half an hour, the older ladies exchanged stories about the childhood antics of sons, grandsons, and nephews.

When it was time to leave, the Duchess invited the whole party to dine at Denton the following week.

~~MrsB~~

Over the next weeks, and then years to come, Mr David Bryant became a frequent visitor, ostensibly visiting Richard Cartwright, but always making time, to drop in at Denton Manor.

If he spent an inordinate amount of time with Alistair and Robert, the only complaint was from the boys, when he left.

Then an uncle of Mr Bryant's died and left him a small, but very viable estate. Providentially for everyone, it was but five and twenty miles from Denton Manor.

~~MrsB~~

During those years, Lady Francine became an expert at British battles, since the boys developed a taste for recreating battles with toy soldiers.

To keep up with their insatiable appetite for new and exciting stories, the Duchess hired a tutor to instruct her daughter in British history. Initially, the middle-aged gentleman was reluctant to teach a girl. After all, young ladies had no need to know about such violent things as battles. But eventually, he became reconciled to the idea since his student took the subject seriously.

Unlike some of his previous male students, Francine took to her studies with great enthusiasm. It opened the world for her. Due to the conventions, many activities and interests allowed to boys and men were considered most improper for young ladies. She, therefore, enjoyed the opportunity to explore ideas not usually allowed her sex.

~~MrsB~~

5 *Young Love*

1787

'Francine, I have something to discuss with you,' the Duchess told her daughter. When her daughter looked expectantly at her, she continued, 'next week I will be taking you to Hertfordshire. You remember I told you of my estate there?'

'Yes, Mama. Netherfield Park, is it not?'

'You are correct. One day the estate will be yours, and I wish to show it to you and introduce you to the staff there. I want them to know you. So that if you ever need to avail yourself of its facilities, you will not have any problems.'

'What is the neighbourhood like, Mama?' Francine was curious.

'They are nice people. A little rustic maybe, since most of them spend the majority of their time in a very restricted community and do not go to town much, but they are generally good people. Netherfield also has the advantage that it is only four and twenty miles from London. Most of it on good roads. You can be in London in only four hours.'

'Can we go to London too? I would love to go to the theatre,' Francine pleaded.

'You want to visit London to go to the theatre? What about the modiste? Would you not like some new dresses?' teased her mother.

'I never go anywhere where I would need fancy dresses. It will be soon enough when I need them for my first season. In the meantime, I prefer to be comfortable,' came the logical reply.

'Very well, we will go to London. We will visit the theatre if you agree to be fitted for three new dresses. After all, I cannot appear at the theatre with you looking like a hoyden,' the Duchess compromised.

~~MrsB~~

Their arrival at Netherfield caused quite a stir. They arrived with three carriages, one for themselves, including Anne Hopkins, one for their staff and one for the luggage.

The Duchess had written ahead for preparations to be made for their visit and to engage extra staff, since most of the time, the house was looked after by a skeleton staff.

The senior staff were assembled in front of the house to greet their Mistress. After a footman assisted them from their coach, the Duchess greeted the butler and the housekeeper, who in turn presented the other staff.

Lady Francine was quite impressed by their manners which were better than she had expected. After all, the family was rarely in residence, and this was a rural community. Then she stopped to look at the house. 'Mama, this is lovely. It looks elegant and yet inviting.'

The Duchess was pleased with this reaction. 'Wait until you see the inside before you get too enthusiastic.'

'I am certain it will be wonderful. Such a lovely exterior must have a beautiful interior.'

The Duchess laughed, 'shall we go, and see?' taking her daughter's arm and leading her inside.

They went inside and looked at a few rooms on their way upstairs to their own chambers where preparations had been made for them to refresh themselves and wash off the travel dust.

An hour later, the Duchess collected Lady Francine for a tour of the house.

Francine was enthusiastic, 'I was right, the interior is even better than the outside. I am not certain how to describe it, but there is a restful quality about this house. I could stay here forever.'

~~MrsB~~

Over the next few days, mother and daughter explored the estate. Inside the house, the Duchess and the housekeeper, Mrs Nicholls, helped Lady Francine become familiar with the house and the staff.

Outside they explored mostly in company of the steward, Mr Thompson. He introduced them to the tenants and escorted them on tours of the grounds.

On one such outing, while riding along the boundary line to their nearest neighbouring estate, Longbourn, they encountered a young man on the other side of the fence, who greeted Mr Thompson with good cheer. 'Good morning, Mr Thompson. Is it not a beautiful day for a ride?'

'Good day to you too, Mr Bennet. I was not aware you had returned from Oxford,' responded Thompson, who then glanced questioningly at the Duchess. When she gave an inviting nod, he continued, 'Your Grace, may I introduce to you Mr Thomas Bennet. He is the second son of Mr Henry Bennet, your neighbour and the Master of Longbourn.' Then he turned to Bennet, 'Mister Bennet, I have the honour to introduce to you, Her Grace, the Duchess of Denton and her daughter Lady Francine Flinter.'

'Your Grace, Lady Francine, it is indeed an unexpected honour to make your acquaintance.' Thomas Bennet politely acknowledged the introduction.

The ladies both responded graciously, then the Duchess continued, 'It has been many years since I had a chance for an extended visit. How are your parents?'

'They are well, Your Grace, they will be excited to hear that you have taken up residence again.'

'In that case, I must ask them to join us for tea.'

~~MrsB~~

A few days later, after the invitation had been issued, Mr and Mrs Bennet, and their two sons, Henry and Thomas, called on the Duchess for tea.

During the general polite enquiries after family, Mr Henry Bennet senior mentioned that Thomas had just completed his education at Oxford and was due to return there in the fall, to teach.

'What subjects will you be teaching Mister Bennet?' Lady Francine enquired.

'My official duties will be to teach history and literature, my lady. But I might tutor some students in other subjects, such as science,' he replied, smiling.

'If you teach literature, does that mean you enjoy reading? What are your favourite books?'

Mr Bennet senior teased, 'he certainly enjoys reading. I always have trouble, getting his nose out of a book.'

'I admit, I can get lost in a good book. One of my favourites is *Robinson Crusoe*. Although I also quite enjoy some of the classics, like the *Iliad*.'

'In the original Greek or the English translation?' Francine was curious.

'It does depend on my mood. If I want to enjoy the subtleties of the story, I read the original Greek.' Then he smiled mischievously, 'and sometimes when I just like to read an exciting tale, I read the English translation.'

Francine laughed delightedly, 'I feel the same way about French, but I would not describe *The Book of the City of Ladies* by Christine de Pizan as an exciting tale. Although I think Madame de Villeneuve's *Beauty and the Beast* a charming story.'

At this point, they were drawn into the general conversation again.

Eventually, as it was time to leave, Mrs Bennet cleared her throat and somewhat self-consciously asked, 'Your Grace, would it be terribly presumptuous, to extend an invitation to dinner to you, both of you?'

The Duchess smiled, 'not at all, Mrs Bennet. I have thoroughly enjoyed our conversation. If I were to follow strict adherence to ranks, I would never be in company. Especially company I enjoy. But you are aware that Francine is not yet out in society?'

'Madam, I doubt anyone from London will find out that in the country our adherence to protocol is not quite so strictly observed.'

~~MrsB~~

Over dinner, they all enjoyed a lively conversation.

At one point, the Duchess jokingly complained to Mrs Bennet, 'Francine would like to explore everything in a day, whereas I do not possess her energy anymore to go traipsing about the countryside all day, every day.'

Thomas immediately offered, 'I would be most happy to accompany Lady Francine and show her the area.'

The Duchess considered the offer for a moment and looked to her daughter for her reaction. Seeing Francine's smile, she agreed. 'Your offer is very kind and much appreciated by me. But we must observe the proprieties. Therefore, I will send my companion to accompany you. She is a good rider.'

~~MrsB~~

The following morning Thomas Bennet arrived at Netherfield Park shortly after breakfast. He was shown into the morning room where the Duchess and Lady Francine were sitting with Mrs Anne Hopkins, the Duchess's companion.

After the greetings and introductions, Lady Francine asked teasingly, 'Where shall we go today, Mr Bennet? What enticing itinerary have you mapped out for us?'

'I thought we could explore the northern boundary of Netherfield Park, then look at the park that gave the estate its name and finally climb Oakham Mount from where you can see all of your estate,' suggested Thomas Bennet.

The Duchess agreed. 'That seems like a good plan. We have not yet explored that area. Mrs Hopkins will accompany you, as well as a groom to look after the horses.'

They followed his suggestion at a leisurely pace, until, two hours later, they finally stopped at the top of Oakham Mount. They dismounted and left the horses with the groom. Mrs Hopkins was content to sit on a fallen log to rest where she could still see her charge but gave her the opportunity to speak privately.

Thomas Bennet escorted Lady Francine to the edge of the plateau, from where they could see Netherfield Park laid out below them.

Lady Francine delighted at the view before her. 'Thank you for bringing me here. The view is simply glorious.' Looking around her for a place to sit, she noticed a large rock which appeared to have been placed perfectly for that purpose. 'I would like to rest for a little while. No matter what my mother claims, I do not wish to spend all day in the saddle. Occasionally I like a seat that holds still,' she smiled.

'By all means, let us sit and admire the view.' Glancing back at Mrs Hopkins and the groom, he remarked, 'I believe our companions are of the same opinion.'

They sat quietly for a little while until Lady Francine could not contain her curiosity any longer. 'Mr Bennet, what is Oxford like? I mean the school, studying, teaching...'

'I do not yet know about teaching, as I have only just finished my own studies, but I have tutored some of my fellow students when they had difficulties in subjects which came easy to me,' he explained. Then he told her of his experiences as a student and what he hoped the future would hold for him.

'I can imagine nothing better than to take a young mind and fill it with knowledge. Provide them with the tools to think, present them with new ideas. Open their minds to possibilities and then watch those minds grow into new directions nobody has thought of before. It is glorious,' Thomas enthused. Then he suddenly realised how he had been speaking. 'My apologies Lady Francine for rambling on so. I am afraid I was quite carried away.'

'Please, Mr Bennet. There is no need to apologise. I think it wonderful how committed you are to your profession. Most men of my acquaintance are content to idle their life away. It is refreshing to speak to someone with a purpose. Someone who means to make a difference.'

~~MrsB~~

Their outings became a regular occurrence over the next few weeks. They often took a picnic lunch and stopped to eat at various scenic spots. Mrs Hopkins, while always present, made a point of giving them enough privacy, to speak freely.

On this occasion, Thomas Bennet waxed lyrical about his love of history.

'I wish I could have had you as my tutor these last three years,' Francine lamented. 'My tutor had not the gift to make the subject as interesting as you do. I only persevered because my nephews love to re-enact battles with their toy soldiers. Mr Cobbins was also very conservative. He felt that young ladies should not disturb their minds with things that are so unsuitable to the tender sensitivities of the female mind.' She mimicked Mr Cobbins with the last part of her speech.

'Why should history be unsuitable to ladies?' Thomas Bennet wondered. 'I believe everyone should learn as much as they can. It makes for a much more interesting conversation.'

As they were speaking, Francine watched the young man. He was very handsome, and when he became enthusiastic about his subject, he became more animated. He forgot his careful manners and propriety, and simply spoke from the heart. To her, that was very endearing.

As a matter of fact, the more she saw of him and came to know him, the more she liked Thomas Bennet. Yes, he was handsome, but his mind was what attracted her even more. He was flexible, not like that stodgy old history tutor she had studied with. He did not show any disfavour to women wanting to learn too.

Then there was the passion with which he spoke about teaching or books or history. She wanted to listen to him for hours. Francine felt he would be good company not just for those hours, but for a lifetime...

Francine caught herself at that thought. She could not possibly consider him as a husband. Or could she?

Would her parents approve? She felt confident that her mother would give her blessing, but her father...

No, she must not let those foolish thoughts continue. She must not.

~~MrsB~~

Thomas Bennet, unbeknownst to Lady Francine, was thinking along similar lines.

He relished the ease of their conversation. He could speak about any subject and knew she would understand. She might not have an in-depth knowledge of some subjects, but she was remarkably well-read. He could imagine evenings spent in conversation. A meeting of minds. And more than just minds...

Thomas longed to reach out to Francine. His half-raised hand was stopped, not by the presence of their chaperone, but by the comprehension that her family would never accept him.

He might be able to convince her mother, but her father had a reputation of being very conscious of status. He would never allow Thomas Bennet to marry his daughter.

He aborted the movement and with an internal sigh, consigned himself to get his feelings back under control.

At that time, he did not fully realise how accurate his conjecture was.

~~MrsB~~

The Duke of Denton arrived at Netherfield Park unannounced. His first order of business was to speak to his wife.

'I have received some troubling reports,' he started after greeting his wife.

'Madam, I have allowed you to raise your daughter as you wish. But I will not allow my daughter to become entangled with someone of no consequence. What use is a daughter, who will squander herself on some commoner.'

The Duchess tried to interrupt, but the Duke held up his hand to stop her. 'I am fully aware, he is distantly related to the Standbys, but he has no real connections and no political influence. Francine will only make an alliance, of which I approve. This commoner I do not approve of. Do I make myself clear?' The Duke spoke without heat, but he brooked no opposition.

'You will make your farewells and pack. You and Francine will return to my estate in two days. I will remain, to ensure you will do as I bid,' the Duke finished.

The Duchess was inwardly fuming at being ordered about like a servant or a recalcitrant child, but she knew that there was no point in arguing when her husband had made up his mind. 'Very well, Denton. We will be ready to leave on Thursday,' she sighed.

Now that she had agreed, the Duke softened a little. 'I want Francine to have everything to which her heritage entitles her. I do not wish for her to live in some squalid little hovel, with a husband who cannot afford to look after her, the way she deserves.'

The Duchess could not restrain herself. 'Netherfield Park is not a squalid little hovel!' she exclaimed.

'I also do not wish for her to fall for some fortune-hunter. If a man cannot support her on his own merits, he cannot have her. And that is final.' With that statement, the Duke turned his back on her and left the room.

~~MrsB~~

The following day, the Duchess, Lady Francine, and Mrs Hopkins paid a farewell visit to Longbourn.

While the Duchess was having tea with Mrs Bennet, Mrs Hopkins suggested that she would enjoy a walk in the garden. Both Lady Francine and Thomas Bennet thought it an excellent idea and joined her. When they were furthest from the house, Mrs Hopkins became quite engrossed for several minutes in examining the flowers. Francine and Thomas stayed within view, but not earshot of the lady. The young man turned to Lady Francine and took her hand in both of his.

'I am most distressed that you are leaving so soon,' he started hesitatingly. 'I had so hoped you would stay longer. Much longer, in fact.' He looked into her lovely blue eyes, trying to convey a message he longed to speak. 'I shall miss you quite dreadfully.'

'I shall miss you too. Your company, over the last few weeks, has been most... amiable. I wish to thank you for the time you have spent showing me your world. It has been most... enlightening.' Francine blushed but gathered her courage and looked Thomas in the eye. 'I truly wish that I could stay. But my father insists that I must leave. It has been wonderful, knowing you.' She swallowed but could not continue.

Thomas Bennet bowed and placed a soft kiss in the palm of Lady Francine's hand. 'I shall never forget you.'

When he straightened, he saw her blushing furiously, with a tremulous smile on her lips.

They both jumped a little when Mrs Hopkins declared, 'ah yes, it is as I thought. This is a very lovely specimen of a tea rose.' She turned around. 'My apologies, I became engrossed in admiring this lovely rose,' she smiled. 'But I am afraid I have kept you out here for too long. Let us return to the parlour.'

She walked beside Francine, who had taken the arm offered by Thomas, as they walked back to the house.

The ladies made their final farewells to the Bennets. They were all rather dispirited when they left Netherfield Park the next day.

~~MrsB~~

6 *London Season*

1789

The London Season had only just begun. The second major ball was being held by the Duke and Duchess of Denton to introduce their daughter, Lady Francine, to society. A few days earlier the young lady had been formally presented at court. Now it was her time to officially make her way onto the marriage mart.

The last few weeks had been frantically busy for the Duchess and her daughter. Despite Lady Francine's disinterest in such things, she had spent considerable time at the modiste's choosing and being fitted for a new wardrobe. Anne Hopkins, the Duchess' companion had been of great support to both ladies, for she had a knack for calming and distracting Francine when she wanted to quit the whole affair.

Her father had presented her with a list of men, whom he considered suitable. Francine was to try to get to know them.

Anne Hopkins gave Francine a different list. She had listed the gossip from the servants about the men who might only be interested in Lady Francine's dowry.

Unsurprisingly almost half the men on her father's list were also on Anne's list.

'Why are those men on father's list?' Francine asked her mother. 'I distinctly remember you telling me that he would not approve of a fortune-hunter marrying me.'

'From what I can gather, those men or their fathers were very discreet about their finances. But servants, who need to find a new position, will talk. Maybe only to other servants, but they will talk. And most members of the nobility would not demean themselves, by asking a servant for an opinion,' interjected Mrs Hopkins.

'It is fortunate indeed, that I am not most members,' quipped the Duchess with a grin.

~~MrsB~~

Now, in her finest ballgown she stood beside her parents greeting guests as they arrived.

The Duke welcomed the latest arrivals. 'Lord Matlock, Lady Matlock, it is good of you to come. May I introduce my daughter Francine? Francine, I would like you to know the Earl and the Countess of Matlock.'

Francine curtsied. 'It is a great pleasure to meet you, Lord Matlock, Lady Matlock.'

The Earl of Matlock bowed. 'I am delighted to meet you, Lady Francine. I have heard much about you from your mother,' he smiled.

'Only good things,' his wife interjected with a smile. 'I also am pleased to make your acquaintance.' She nodded at Francine.

Francine nodded in return and replied with a slight smile, 'please keep in mind that my mother is biased.'

~~MrsB~~

The Duke opened the dancing with his daughter. For his age, he was still in good shape, and he had always been a handsome man. The years had made him only more distinguished looking. They made a remarkably handsome couple on the dancefloor.

After the first set with her father, Lady Francine was inundated with requests for dances. She had to disappoint many potential suitors.

She had looked forward to the dancing, as it was an exercise she enjoyed immensely. Her mother had hired excellent musicians; therefore, she had nothing to complain about on that score. She laughed at herself for that horrible pun while smiling politely.

Unfortunately, the conversation with her dance partners left much to be desired. Between discussions of the weather for possibly all of the last year and the excessive flattery, her polite smile became exceedingly difficult to maintain.

~~MrsB~~

'All that these men are interested in are father and my dowry. None of them listens to me when I venture an opinion. I could just scream.' Lady Francine was pacing in her sitting room at Denton House.

Her mother and Anne Hopkins were sitting in chairs by the window enjoying the weak sunshine.

'How can they be both simpering and patronising at the same time?'

'It is called flattering not simpering,' corrected her mother, while suppressing an amused smile. 'At least, when a man does it.'

'You can call it whatever you like. I hate it.' Francine did not usually indulge in tantrums, but she had been pushed to what she perceived to be her limits.

'*Lady Francine, you have such lovely eyes. I am certain, your children will be celebrated for their beauty*, and I am not even engaged yet,' Francine fumed. 'Especially not to that fop.'

'Then there was that second son of Baron Watsonever, who insisted that my dancing was as delicate as a butterfly wafting from bloom to bloom. Does that puppy think father would ever consider him as suitable?'

'And of course, there was Viscount Stoner, who tried so very hard to get me to admire the view from the deserted balcony. Does he not know that the servants who his father had to let go because he cannot afford to pay them, would pass on the gossip about his desperation for money? My dowry would be gone the day after the wedding. And then I would be stuck with that rake.'

'My dear, no one from the nobility would possibly listen to servants' gossip.' Mrs Hopkins said in the most supercilious tone before breaking into a wide smile.

'Was there anyone you liked?' Her mother asked, getting slightly exasperated.

'Baron Standby was rather fun to converse with,' she started. At her mother's raised eyebrow, she sighed and continued, 'yes, I know, he is not on father's list. But at least with him I get some relief from the tedium.' She now looked wistful, remembering a particular cousin of the Baron's.

'Mother, if I am not allowed to marry for love, at least I want a man of good character and mutual respect.' Francine, having exhausted her nervous energy, sank into the final chair. 'In the meantime, I will smile and dance and hope that there is at least one man I can live with.'

~~MrsB~~

Earl Fellmar was in a foul mood. He had come to the ball specifically to woo Lady Francine. But somehow, he could not get close to her. There was always someone who distracted him just long enough that she was back on the dancefloor before he had an opportunity to ask her for a dance.

When at long last he did manage to approach her and ask for a dance, her dance-card was full.

He should not have been surprised. After all, she was the prime catch of the current season. At the age of seventeen, she had only recently been presented and was already highly sought after.

As the daughter of the Duke of Denton as well as the Duchess, who herself was the daughter of the Duke of Brastone, she had all the connections for which one could wish. The Duke was also known to be wealthy, and her dowry was rumoured to be thirty thousand pounds.

The fact that she was beautiful besides being tall, willowy, blond, and blue-eyed appealed to him as well. She was very much the type he liked to play with.

Since he was very discreet, society was unaware of his tastes. He enjoyed inflicting pain, as his first wife found out nearly twenty years ago. She too had been tall and blond. Unfortunately, he had been too young to learn proper control.

He had pushed his wife too far while she was carrying their first child and, in her panic, to escape him, she had tripped and fallen all the way down the grand staircase. Her broken neck was determined by the doctor to be the cause of death. Fortunately for his reputation, her bruises were also attributed to the fall. They had only been married for six months. Everyone commiserated with him for his misfortune.

Since then, he had become more careful and more subtle.

When he married again five years later, his second wife lasted for two years. The day after giving birth to his son and heir, he had enjoyed himself with her, despite her pleas. He had not enjoyed the next morning when he found his son smothered and his wife had hanged herself. Luckily only he had seen and read the note which said, '*I will not inflict another monster on this world*.'

Again, everyone had sympathised with him. It was unfortunate that some women became unhinged after giving birth, some of his associates tutted.

Now he needed another wife. One with a dowry sufficient to allow him to clear his debts and continue with his chosen lifestyle. And one who could give him a much-needed heir.

Although he was not prepared to reform completely, this time he was determined to restrain himself enough, that his heir would survive. After all, if he were to die without an heir his title and the estate would go to a cousin whom he despised.

Lady Francine appeared to be perfect for him. Titled, well connected, wealthy, beautiful as well as young and healthy. Now he just needed to convince her and her father that he was perfect for her.

At the age of eight and thirty, he was still in good shape due to all the exercise he enjoyed. He was reasonably good looking, although his lack of hair, while it bothered him, was convenient under the wigs he wore. He considered himself to be in the prime of his life.

Luckily for the Earl, knowledge of his debts was restricted to a very limited group of people, and he was also very active in politics. This activity often put him in company with the Duke of Denton.

Although the Duke was not at the ball, Fellmar planned to speak to him on the subject of his daughter.

~~MrsB~~

7 Marriage - Bennet

1789

In the summer of 1789, Thomas Bennet came for a visit to his family. He was greeted with great enthusiasm by his mother and more restrained fondness by his father and older brother.

While he enjoyed his position as a teacher at Oxford, it was good to spend time in the country again with all the familiar faces and places of his childhood. His mother fussed over him being concerned that while on his own he could not possibly be eating enough and that he had no one to look after him.

He tried to reassure her, 'I have very nice rooms at Oxford, and Mrs Salford is an excellent landlady who sets a good table.'

'Perhaps that is so,' conceded his mother. 'But while you are here, I will get a chance to *ensure* you are properly looked after.'

'Very well, mother. I will put myself in your hands,' Thomas laughed. 'Is there any other little thing I can do to make you happy?'

'As a matter of fact, there is something. You can come to the assembly tonight. Your arrival today is most fortuitous. Lately, we have been woefully short of gentlemen for the young ladies to dance with.' Mrs Bennet smiled while she hoped that a young lady would capture his attention. Her older son Henry had proven to be remarkably disinterested in the young ladies. He was always in company with his male friends. She simply could not understand his attitude.

She was getting to the point where she truly pined for grandchildren. Since her older son was disinclined to indulge her, she hoped that her younger son would soon provide an heir for the estate. He seemed to have overcome his infatuation with Lady Francine. As much as she had thought the young lady quite pleasant, Mrs Bennet had had no illusions about the lady's father allowing such a match.

'An assembly tonight, you say? My arrival was well-timed then. I do enjoy a dance.' Thomas smiled at his mother. 'In that case, I had better wash up thoroughly before tonight.'

~~MrsB~~

Thomas Bennet was very popular at the assembly that evening. He had been absent for six months and was welcomed back wholeheartedly.

He danced every set. Each with a different partner, most of whom he knew from previous years. There was one new face amongst the young ladies with which he was not familiar. She was introduced to him by his mother as Miss Francine Gardiner.

He attempted not to show it, but both her appearance and her name struck a chord with him. Her looks and her manner, which was an odd combination of lively yet demure reminded him of Lady Francine. He was most intrigued and determined to get to know her better.

Over the next few weeks, he assiduously attended teas, dinners, card-parties, and yet another assembly.

He met Miss Gardiner at many of these events. He suspected his mother, who had noted his interest, arranged for invitations to include both of them. He took full advantage of the opportunities presented to them to get to know more about her.

Miss Gardiner had only recently come out into society. She was sweet and demure, she almost always spoke in a gentle voice, but she had a tinkling laugh which made him think of silver bells. When they conversed, she listened to him most attentively. She was also accomplished in many of the things young ladies were expected to be accomplished in.

To put it simply, he was captivated. He admitted to himself, and only to himself, that Miss Francine Gardiner was no Lady Francine, but she was attainable rather than the dream he had two years earlier.

Just before he was due to return to Oxford, he escorted Miss Gardiner on a walk around the country lanes while her younger sister and a maid chaperoned them. While their chaperones kept them in sight, they fell behind far enough to allow them to speak in private.

He was grateful that the other pair dawdled not realising this was by design rather than by chance. After trying to make some banal conversation for a few minutes, Miss Gardiner turned to Thomas and asked ingeniously, 'is something the matter Mr Bennet? You seem quite discomposed today.'

Taking that as the opening he had been hoping for, Thomas replied, 'yes, Miss Gardiner, something is discomposing me. That something is you. Please allow me to tell you that I have quite fallen in love with you. Your beauty, your poise and your charm have quite captured my heart.'

They had stopped beside some sweet-smelling flowering shrubs. He turned to Francine and taking her hands asked the question she had been hoping for. 'Miss Gardiner, would you do me the honour to become my wife.'

'Yes, Mr Bennet, I would be delighted,' Francine Gardiner smiled brightly.

'Thank you, Miss Gardiner. You have made me very happy.' He raised her hands and lightly kissed the back of them. 'May I presume on our betrothal and use your given name when in private?'

'You may if I am also permitted to use yours,' she smiled at him.

'Most certainly, I would love to hear my name on your lips,' Thomas conceded. 'But now, I believe, I had better go and see your father to ask his permission.'

~~MrsB~~

Thomas Bennet went to see Mr Gardiner to ask for and receive permission to marry Miss Francine Gardiner.

The happy couple agreed on a wedding date of Monday, December 14, when Thomas would be back from Oxford for the holidays.

They would spend Christmas with their families and relocate to Oxford immediately afterwards. This would allow them time to settle into their new home together before Thomas Bennet had to take up his teaching duties again in the new year.

~~MrsB~~

Thomas Bennet arrived back from Oxford on the 12th of December. As soon as he had greeted his family, he rushed into Meryton to see his intended.

He could hardly wait to see her again. Although they had corresponded, it was not the same. He had written to her about his work and students, while her letters had been filled with excitement about the wedding preparations. Although he had not been present, by now he knew every detail about the colour scheme of the decorations, the flowers, the invitations, and the menu for the wedding breakfast.

Now he hoped they would be able to speak about other things, like their future or his work. Alas, when he arrived at the Gardiner residence, the ladies were still too preoccupied with the upcoming wedding to have any thought for ought else.

But he did manage to share a brief moment with his bride to be.

'Oh, Thomas, I can hardly wait. Only two more days until our wedding. How happy we shall be. What wonderful times we shall have. I cannot wait to move to Oxford with you,' she smiled coyly. 'But now, I must rush. There is still so much to be done to finish my trousseau. I want everything to be perfect.' She gave him a brilliant smile.

He gave in to her enthusiasm and let her get back to her preparations. It made him feel good to see her so excited and eager to become his wife. He smiled indulgently. 'Just so, my love. I am just as impatient as you are. I will not keep you from your preparations.' He raised her hands to his lips and kissed them. 'Only two more days.'

~~MrsB~~

Monday morning dawned bright and clear. There had been a slight snowfall overnight which turned the landscape into a magical wonderland. Thomas Bennet could barely contain his excitement. Today, the lovely Francine would become his wife.

He waited at the altar, with his brother Henry beside him. His eyes were fixed on the entrance until at last his bride walked in on the arm of her father. To him she was a vision in palest pink with pink flowers in her hair. She looked absolutely radiant.

When they reached Thomas, Mr Gardiner placed Francine's hand in his. After that, the whole ceremony was a blur for him. He must have responded correctly at the right times, but he could not remember any of the details. Eventually, they signed the register and were presented to the assembled family and friends, as Mr and Mrs Thomas Bennet.

They adjourned to Longbourn for the wedding breakfast since there was more space for the guests. There was delicious food, toasts, and speeches, some serious and some good-naturedly teasing.

Eventually, the happy couple made their farewells and took up residence in a cottage which Mr Henry Bennet senior had arranged, as a wedding present for the newlyweds to spend the Christmas holidays. A woman would arrive every morning to look after them and prepare meals.

Thomas Bennet approached his bride with all the tenderness of which he was capable. Francine was grateful that he was gentle with her since she remembered her mother's instruction to hold still and let her husband do as he wished. It was supposed to be an unpleasant duty which she would have to endure until she was with child. To her misfortune, she focused so hard on doing her duty, that she had not a chance to relax and experience the pleasure that she might otherwise have had.

Francine decided, therefore, that although the experience was not as painful as she had expected, she would acquiesce to her husband's demands as little as possible.

Thomas was a little disappointed at the lack of response. But he consoled himself with the idea that his wife might just need a little time to become comfortable with the intimate side of their relationship.

~~MrsB~~

Since they were now family, the Bennets had invited the Gardiners to spend Christmas Day at Longbourn.

After church services in the morning, both families adjourned to Longbourn where a Christmas feast awaited them. It was a very merry party with the younger Gardiners singing Christmas carols. Fifteen-year-old Martha and eighteen-year-old Edward had good voices, which blended in a lovely harmony.

If things were a little strained between the newlyweds, everyone put it down to impatience to be gone from the gathering.

~~MrsB~~

Two days after Christmas, the Bennets left their honeymoon cottage. Since the journey to Oxford could be achieved in one day, if one left Meryton early in the morning, the couple decided to do just that.

Mr and Mrs Thomas Bennet travelled to Oxford in the Bennet carriage, which Mr Bennet senior had lent them to ease the bride's relocation.

When they arrived at the boarding house where Thomas Bennet had his rooms, Francine Bennet was thrilled at the grandeur of the building.

'Oh, Mr Bennet, is this where we will live? I never expected to be Mistress of such a grand house,' she excitedly exclaimed.

'My dear, remember when I told you I rented rooms in a boarding house...'

'Yes, I remember, but now that we are married you have rented for us a magnificent property,' his wife interrupted.

'No, my dear, I did not. This is the boarding house I was telling you about. Our rooms are on the first floor,' Thomas explained.

Francine's face fell. 'Oh, how you vex me, Mr Bennet. I thought that as a married man, you would arrange for your own house to which to bring your wife.'

'I did arrange for a larger set of rooms than the ones I used to occupy,' Thomas Bennet explained. 'Why do we not go inside, and you can see how pleasant the apartment is.' He took her hand and put it in the crook of his arm.

When they entered the foyer, the landlady, Mrs Salford, bustled out to greet them. 'Mr Bennet, welcome back. Is this your lovely wife? How pretty she is,' the middle-aged lady exclaimed. 'Welcome home, Mrs Bennet. If you need anything or if you just want some female company, come down to see me any time you like.'

After the greeting, Mr Bennet led his bride up to their rooms. They entered a large and airy sitting room. 'There are bedrooms to either side, and each also has a dressing room. I thought you should have the larger of the rooms because the smaller also has a small study, which I will need to use when I tutor students.'

'You bring students to our home?' young Mrs Bennet asked incredulously. 'Why would you do such a thing?'

'Since my salary is still small, I tutor students for the extra money,' explained Mr Bennet patiently.

'Are you telling me you are poor?' Francine asked, her voice rising. 'I thought professors earned a great deal of money.'

'Established professors can earn a very comfortable income, but I am just starting out.'

'Why did you not tell me?! You married me under false pretences.'

'But I did tell you about it when you asked me about my life in Oxford.'

'Oh dear. I suppose I was not listening.' Francine was chagrined. Her mother had warned her about her habit of not paying attention. But she had assumed that as a gentleman, even as a second son, Mr Bennet would be well established. She had looked forward to being Mistress of her own home. And by a home, she meant a house. Not an apartment in a boarding house. No matter how pleasant.

She had expected a life of ease and plenty. Now her expectations were dashed. This was another disagreeable shock to her.

It possibly made her next responses more honest than she had intended, when her husband asked, 'when I was courting you, did you listen to anything I said?'

'Not if I could help it. Why would I. You always rattled on about various boring characters from old books.'

Thomas Bennet was stunned. What he had taken for silent admiration, had simply been an empty-headed stare.

~~MrsB~~

Thomas Bennet despaired. At the age of three and twenty, he was tied for life to a vain and vapid creature, who always claimed he vexed her when she was vexation personified.

Instead of the relaxed and contended harmony to which he had looked forward, he now was stuck with a verbose and shrill termagant.

She also could not practice economy. He was constantly having to advance money to her to pay for the purchases she commissioned. To add insult to injury, when three weeks after their wedding, her courses did not occur, she declared herself finished with the intimate aspect of their marriage until well after her son was born.

While he was aware that some men demanded their rights, and some even forced the issue, that kind of action was not his way. He had been raised to respect women. He would continue to hold to his principles, even if it killed him.

Since at home, he had no one with whom to converse, he threw himself into his work. He became a most attentive teacher to his students. A few of them, who were interested in learning, benefitted from this attention.

At home, he and his wife exchanged the barest civilities. He found that Mrs Bennet had befriended Mrs Salford. He was grateful that his landlady was prepared to provide some companionship to his wife. Although as time passed, he noticed Mrs Salford giving him pitying looks more and more often.

~~MrsB~~

Three months later, Francine Bennet felt the quickening. For the first time in weeks, both she and her husband were happy together. Mr Bennet wrote to his parents, informing them of the good news.

Both their parents responded with letters of congratulations and the expectation that theirs must be a felicitous marriage.

Mrs Bennet was in heaven. She was the centre of attention of both families. She received presents in the form of money, with which to buy items she would need for the baby or soft fabrics suitable for a baby's soft and delicate skin. She decided that some of those fabrics would also be delightful for chemises for herself.

~~MrsB~~

8 Master of Longbourn

1790

They had barely settled in the new routine when a devastating letter arrived for Thomas Bennet.

Messrs Henry Bennet senior and junior had been travelling back to Longbourn, when in a freak accident, a tree had fallen and crushed the carriage in which they were riding. The coachman had a few bruises and scrapes where the branches had caught him, but he was otherwise unhurt.

The letter came from Mr Gardiner, who had been Mr Bennet's solicitor. It informed him, that since he was now Master of Longbourn he needed to come home.

~~MrsB~~

Thomas Bennet left his wife in the care of Mrs Salford, to pack up and get ready to move to Longbourn while he rushed back to Meryton to see to the funeral and his mother.

His mother was devastated. She had been married for three decades, and now she missed the strong support her husband had been. They spent an evening comforting each other before Thomas made the final arrangements for his father and brother.

When it came to the funeral, Mrs Bennet insisted she attend. Her male relations attempted to explain that women were considered to be too delicate to attend such sombre affairs. After they took one glance at the look of steel in Mrs Bennet's eyes, it made them hold their tongues and acquiesce to her wishes.

During the funeral Mrs Bennet's spine was ramrod straight despite tears pouring down her cheeks. When the coffins were lowered into the grave, her final tribute was a single perfect white rose which she cast onto the coffins. Then she turned and walked back to Longbourn, silently followed by her maid and a footman.

~~MrsB~~

Two days later Thomas Bennet travelled to Oxford with a maid to collect his wife.

She was attired in a fashionable new gown. At least it was black. He bit back a comment on her spending too much yet again.

Then she complained, 'I did not have enough time or money to have a proper wardrobe made befitting my new station.'

After the upheaval over the last ten days, the funeral and then the exhaustion from his travels, the complaint became too much for Thomas Bennet.

'Madam, it is customary to wear black to show respect for the death of a loved one. It is not an excuse to buy the latest fashions,' he growled. 'I hope that you have arranged to have all our belongings packed, ready to be taken to Longbourn?'

Since his wife could hardly wait to be Mistress of an estate, she had been ready to leave for the past two days. She could not feel any great sadness that her father-in-law had died since she had hardly known the man. But she was ecstatic that she would now be Mistress of Longbourn. She had chosen the right husband after all. But since that husband was in a foul mood at present, she tempered her response.

'Yes, Mr Bennet, everything is packed, and I am ready to leave.'

'Good. Now I would like to refresh myself. Please have the courtesy to have some supper sent up. Then I can eat before getting some rest.'

Mrs Bennet stalked out of the sitting room in a huff.

~~MrsB~~

The next morning Mr Bennet rousted his wife out of bed as soon as it was light.

Mrs Bennet, who was normally a late riser, complained, 'Mr Bennet, why must you wake me at this ungodly hour. The sun has barely risen.'

'Madam, if you remember our journey here from Meryton, you will be aware that it is an all-day journey. Due to your condition, I expect us to make more frequent stops, therefore we will have to leave as soon as you are dressed, and we have broken our fast. I will send the maid to assist you.'

Although she still grumbled, Mrs Bennet did as she was bid.

In a surprisingly short time, the last items were packed, and they were ready to leave.

On his way out he saw Mrs Salford, whom he addressed with a heartfelt, 'thank you, Madam. For every thing.' He bowed over her hand.

She patted his hand in a motherly fashion and replied, 'you are most welcome.'

~~MrsB~~

The journey to Longbourn was arduous for Mrs Bennet. Although she managed to sleep for some time, the constant movement had not agreed with her. At least the frequent stops made the journey easy for the horses.

It was evening when they arrived in the front courtyard and Francine was ready to collapse. Her husband was solicitous as he helped her out of the carriage. By the time she had her feet firmly on the ground Mrs Bennet senior and Mrs Hill were there ready to greet them. Mrs Bennet was concerned when she saw how pale Francine Bennet was.

'My dear, we are so happy you have arrived. Hill has prepared a bath for you to help you relax.' Mrs Bennet embraced her daughter-in-law full of concern. 'Come in and refresh yourself. Is there anything we can get you?'

'No, thank you. A bath would be heavenly right now. Apart from that, I do not need anything else for the moment. Just have my trunks sent to the Mistress's rooms,' Francine requested in a tired and abstracted tone.

Mrs Hill took in a sharp breath then schooled her features. 'I shall ensure that your trunks are sent to your rooms.'

'Thank you.' Francine let herself be led into the house by Mrs Bennet, who escorted her to her bath. A maid followed along to help Francine. Her mother-in-law assured her, 'I will have some clean garments sent to you, and a tray will be waiting in your room when you are ready.'

Francine was too tired to respond; she simply let the maid help her to undress and then gratefully immersed herself in the warm bath. When she was relaxed enough to move again, the maid helped her dry off and don the nightgown and soft robe which had been sent.

When the maid assisted Francine to her room, she was too tired to pay attention to where they were going. She was happy to see the tray with light foods waiting for her. It did not take long for her to eat the supper and then, still in something of a daze, she crawled into bed and fell instantly asleep.

~~MrsB~~

Meanwhile, Thomas Bennet and his mother were having a discussion about the situation in which they found themselves. Upon arrival, he had quickly refreshed himself and eaten the supper prepared for him. Now it was time for him to explain to his mother the true state of his marriage.

'I had wondered if Francine was the right choice for you,' said Mrs Bennet thoughtfully. 'But you seemed so very happy in the beginning.

'I was blinded by her looks, and now I have to make the best of it,' sighed Thomas Bennet.

'Now, what is this about the Mistress' suite? Does Francine expect me to give over my rooms to her when my husband has only just been buried?'

'I am sorry mother. I had no idea she was even thinking about this.'

'Apart from being exceedingly rude and inconsiderate, she is not yet fit to be mistress of an estate. I have the impression that she thinks it is all about status but has no concept of the work involved,' his mother continued.

'To be honest, even I know nothing about running an estate. Since Henry was helping father, we do not even have a steward whom I can consult. I was hoping that you might know more than you admitted to in the past.' He looked expectantly at Mrs Bennet.

For the first time, Mrs Bennet smiled faintly. 'I know the tenants and their problems. I know about what they grow, and which fields are providing a good yield and which ones do not. I can also teach Francine about running the household if she is prepared to listen. For financial matters and contracts, you had better speak to your father-in-law. He handled all the official estate business for your father.'

'I know the tenants if they are still the same,' he looked queryingly at his mother, who nodded. 'But I do not know them well. I would greatly appreciate your help.' Thomas started to relax. He had been worried that he would have to try to figure everything out by himself.

He still had concerns, but at least he would not have to deal with them alone. He realised sadly that he did not consider his wife to be of any help to him.

~~MrsB~~

Francine Bennet was initially disappointed that she would not occupy the Mistress' quarters for the moment. But then she decided that the benefit of not doing so outweighed the vexation.

After all, she had the title but someone else was doing the work. Also, her condition was quite visible by now. She justified her sloth by saying that she was doing the most important job on the estate. She was providing the heir for Longbourn.

She refused to acknowledge that the sex of the child was unknown until the birth. She was determined that she was carrying a son. When discussing names for the child, she and Thomas agreed on the name 'James' for a son. Francine refused to even consider names for girls.

That summer was an extremely uncomfortable time for the Bennet household. The family was in mourning for Mr Bennet senior and Henry Bennet junior. Therefore, they could not go visiting or receive callers, other than family.

Francine Bennet was bored. Due to the mourning customs, she could not show off her new status. As the summer progressed, the heat gave her great discomfort due to her condition. She became even more shrill in her demands.

Thomas Bennet found every excuse not to be in the presence of his wife. When he was not out on the estate, he was in his study on the pretext that he was learning about estate management. The study had a wonderfully thick door which dampened all sounds from the house. This room became his haven.

~~MrsB~~

9 *Compromise*

1790

The Duke of Denton confronted his daughter. 'This is your second season, and you still have not chosen a husband. If you do not decide by the time the season is over, I will decide for you. Fellmar has approached me about you, and he seems a very good match. I know he is not quite as young as the others, but he has looked after himself, and he would be a stabilising influence on you.'

'Father, all these men are interested in is you and my dowry,' protested Lady Francine. 'Not one of them has the slightest interest in myself. I at least want a decent man I can be friends with. After all, I will be tied to him for the rest of my life. But all these men see when they look at me is pounds and coronets. Please, father, give me time,' she pleaded.

She knew that her parents were barely acquainted, but she believed her father to be basically a good man. He was myopic in some respects and a misogynist, but he did want what was best for her. It was simply that their opinions on what was best differed greatly.

'My dear girl, are they truly that bad? Young Standish seems to be quite enamoured with you, and his family is quite well placed. Not as good as I had hoped for, but nonetheless the Viscount will be an Earl one day.'

'I am sorry to disappoint you father, but Viscount Standish is in love with Lady Mary. He is only paying attention to me to further his acquaintance with her.'

'Bother. Since you seemed to like him, I had hoped…' he trailed off.

'I do not know what it is. The men I do not like will not leave me alone. And the ones I can tolerate are always interested in somebody else,' Francine sighed.

'Very well. I will give you a little more time. Not too much, mind you. But a little more will not hurt, I suppose.'

'Thank you, father,' replied a very relieved Lady Francine.

~~MrsB~~

Lady Francine was relieved to be back at Denton Manor. Although it had been only June, the London air had become almost unbearable to her. Now, that July had started, she relished the clean air of Essex and the freedom to ride on their estate.

This morning she had risen very early to enjoy a ride in the crisp morning air. A groom accompanied her to ensure her safety and to look after her horse if she wanted to stop anywhere.

She soon reached her favourite spot on the estate. A small lake with woods on one side and an expansive view of fields on the other. She asked the groom to stay back to allow her some privacy to bathe her feet in the cool water. He was happy to do so, as he had noticed a patch of blueberries a short way back.

After he had gone, she took off her boots and stockings and carefully holding her riding habit out of the way she walked from the gravel beach into the lake to enjoy the cool water on her feet and ankles. She was not paying attention to her surroundings when she was startled by a male voice very close to her.

'My, what a pretty sight. You have lovely ankles,' Earl Fellmar commented appreciatively.

Francine whirled around at the sound, but the loose gravel made her lose her balance and she would have fallen, had Fellmar not grabbed her by the arm, pulling her towards himself.

She tried to regain her composure and said quite severely, 'you should not be here, my Lord. You are being most improper.'

'That is all the thanks I get from saving you from a plunge into the water?' the Earl complained.

'If you had not startled me, I would have been in no danger of a tumble,' Francine protested, trying to pull herself away from him.

'Well, now. What an interesting choice of words. I suppose I will have to give you that tumble after all,' he grinned in anticipation.

'Unhand me, Sir.' Francine was getting worried. 'I will call for help,' she threatened.

'Scream all you like. I saw your groom on my way. He is too far away to hear you. And I shall enjoy your screams.' With those words, he picked her up and threw her onto a grassy patch. 'Let us celebrate our engagement.'

For the next half hour, Lady Francine wished she could die or at least faint.

~~MrsB~~

When Fellmar was finished with her, he told her, 'you now have two choices. One, we will go to your father and tell him that you agreed to marry me. Alternatively, I will spread the word how you threw yourself at me. Option one will only be unpleasant for you. Option two will ruin your family. What is it to be?'

Francine looked at him, horrified. 'You are the vilest man I have ever had the misfortune to meet. You truly expect me to put myself into your power?'

'How will your family react when I tell them how you eagerly lifted your skirts for me?' he mocked.

'They know I would never have done this willingly!' asserted Francine. 'My father knows I do not like you.'

'Methinks the lady protest too much,' Fellmar smirked.

'Oh.' Francine's mind was whirling. Could she convince her parents that he was lying? What if there was a child? Damn him. Based on her knowledge, a child was a distinct possibility. She wanted to scream, to rant in her frustration and anger and hurt, but she was not going to give him that satisfaction as well. But he was correct in his assertion, her stated opposition to him could be taken as unacknowledged interest. In addition, her father was in favour of the match since Fellmar's reputation was not that of a rake. He was obviously exceedingly good at dissembling.

'Exactly. Now, what is it to be?' he gloated.

Lady Francine gathered the courage of generations of noble ancestors around her. 'Very well, I shall marry you.'

~~MrsB~~

Now that he had achieved his goal, Fellmar was quite prepared to play the gentleman. He brought her boots and stockings to her, which she put on pretending a nonchalance she did not feel. He then helped Francine to her feet, a gesture she grudgingly accepted. He even assisted her in straightening her riding habit and brushing off grass and leaves from her back.

'We must not give people reason to think that you have been inappropriate with your intended,' he taunted.

'How considerate of you,' was the sarcastic reply.

'Be careful,' he admonished, 'I will not tolerate an impudent wife.'

Lady Francine swallowed convulsively, then straightened her posture and raised her chin in defiance. 'I expect you will not. But I am not your wife yet.'

'My dear, I will delight in teaching you to be a proper wife,' he laughed.

Francine balled her hands into fists by her side and turned away from him so he would not see the tears which threatened in her eyes. 'I would like to return home now. I am certain that you are impatient to inform my father about our agreement,' she managed to say without looking at him.

~~MrsB~~

The Duke was delighted when Fellmar and Francine announced their wish to marry.

'Francine, I am exceedingly pleased to hear this. But what made you change your mind? Sorry Fellmar, but my daughter only recently told me she would not consider you as a husband.'

Francine answered cryptically with a forced smile, 'I have learnt of the Earl's true character. Therefore, I must have him.'

The Duke, as she had expected, mistook her meaning and asked if they had a date in mind.

Francine, who was well aware of the rhythm of her courses, forced a bright smile and told her happy father, 'now that I have decided, I would like it to be as soon as possible.'

'Very well, we will have the first banns read the day after tomorrow.'

~~MrsB~~

Later that evening, Lady Francine ordered a very hot bath and then dismissed her maid. She wanted no witness while she scrubbed herself nearly raw in a futile attempt to feel clean again. She sobbed while she tried to erase the persistent slime, her mind insisted, was wherever he had touched her. Eventually, the water cooled too much, and she got out of the bath.

She had only just dried off and donned a nightgown and robe when she received a visit from her mother.

The Duchess looked searchingly at her daughter. Being more attuned to Francine than her father was she had noticed the brittleness in her behaviour during the evening and it made her concerned enough to come and see her. Taking her daughter's hands, she asked quietly, 'what happened today to make you change your mind?'

At the sympathy in the question Lady Francine's control broke. She threw herself into her mother's arms and started to sob. In between her sobs, she managed to tell her mother about her experience.

The Duchess was horrified. 'You cannot marry that beast!' she exclaimed.

Francine shook her head. 'I must. Else he will tell the world that I compromised myself. And I will not be able to deny his accusations. Based on what you explained to me and what I have read in those books you hide from father; I will have a child. I just pray it is a daughter, and she will be like myself and not like her father. But I want that child to be acknowledged.' She sighed while she managed to gain control of herself again. 'There is simply no escape. I can only hope that he ignores me most of the time.'

The Duchess reluctantly agreed but then reflected. 'It may not be too bad.' At Francine's startled look, she explained, 'he lost his first wife while she was expecting. His second wife and his heir died just after the birth. Considering his age, he must be desperate for an heir. I happen to know he loathes the cousin who is his current heir. I expect he will restrain himself until he has a living heir and perhaps even until he has a spare. In the meantime, I think you should encourage him to take a mistress.'

'I certainly do not wish for his attentions again if I can help it,' Francine agreed. 'I will do what I can. Thank you, Mama.'

~~MrsB~~

The Duchess left her daughter's rooms in a thoughtful mood. It was obvious to her that her husband was completely unaware of the Earl's character. Even though the Duke was politically motivated when he favoured a match with their daughter, she did not believe he would have wanted Francine to be forced in such a way to accept marriage to such a man.

She decided to speak to her husband on the subject the only time he would be guaranteed not to be in the Earl's company which was now when he was in his rooms. The decision made, she went to her rooms and knocked on the joining door between their suites. She heard the surprise in her husband's voice when he bade her to enter.

'This is an unexpected pleasure,' he smiled at her. 'Have you come for my company or is there another reason? The engagement of our daughter perhaps?'

The Duchess decided on an indirect approach. 'Yes, it is about Francine. Do you know why she agreed to marry Fellmar?'

Her husband looked puzzled. 'I would have expected Francine to be even more forthcoming with you than she was with me. She said she realised what a good man Fellmar is and decided she wanted to marry him.'

The Duchess looked sceptical. 'Pray tell, what were her precise words. Not your interpretation of them.'

'If I remember correctly, she said that she had discovered Fellmar's true character, and therefore, she had to have him. What is so difficult to understand?' The Duke was getting rather exasperated with his wife's questioning.

'Francine discovered his true character, but his character is not what you think. That vile man raped our daughter,' the Duchess spat. If looks could kill and Fellmar had been present, he would have breathed his last.

The Duke looked stunned. 'I am certain my dear, that Francine must be mistaken. Certainly, even a chaste kiss might be a little overwhelming for an innocent girl, but that could hardly be called rape,' he protested.

His wife's anger was now directed at him. 'I have seen the bruises he left all over her body. That was no chaste kiss. And then he had the hide to suggest, that if she did not consent to marry him, he would ruin her reputation and ours in the process. That is the character she discovered,' she glared.

The Duke looked stunned. 'Are you quite confident of your assertions?' he asked in disbelief. At his wife's disgusted look, he sighed, 'you are convinced. Oh, my dear lord, I never wanted that for the dear child. Yes, I wanted her to make an advantageous marriage, but to a man who would treat her with respect. I thought Fellmar was such a man. Is there any way we can circumvent this?'

The Duchess took a deep breath to calm herself before she responded, 'no, there is not. She expects to have a child from this encounter; therefore, she will be obliged to marry him. But when you discuss the settlement with that beast, keep in mind that I will not gift Francine with Netherfield as part of her dowry. I will keep that in trust for her if she ever is in need of a refuge.'

Her husband looked shaken. 'That is a good plan. But in all other respects, I believe we should not indicate in any way that we are aware of the situation. It would not do if he thought he has the upper hand.' He became more thoughtful. 'I will have to consider how best to protect Francine from him in the future.'

'Find him a mistress who enjoys pain,' was the blunt reply from his wife.

Looking a little startled, but more hopeful the Duke replied, 'I may know of someone who might suit. I will have to make enquiries.'

~~MrsB~~

10 Marriage - Fellmar

1790

Three weeks later, with all the pomp and ceremony which can be arranged in such a short time with the funds available to the Duke, Lady Francine Flinter prepared to become the Countess Fellmar. Since, as she expected, her courses had not arrived the previous week, she lost her last hope of avoiding the marriage.

Invitations had been sent far and wide, promoting the whirlwind romance of the engaged couple. Many of the invitations had been accepted, and the guests had arrived the day before.

The wedding would take place in the private chapel at Denton. The Duke's cousin, Bishop Flinter, had agreed to perform the ceremony.

Now Lady Francine was getting ready. She had donned the beautiful new gown of blue silk, which had been made for her. The Duchess gifted her with a set of jewellery, consisting of a diamond and sapphire necklace with matching bracelet and earrings. This magnificent set complemented the gown.

The Duke's gift was priceless. A hug and the whispered words, 'I'm sorry'. Those words nearly brought Francine undone, as she clung to her father for a moment.

Then she let go of him, straightened her shoulders, and raised her head. She would meet her fate as the proud daughter of an ancient house. Not the cowed creature, her soon to be husband was trying to make her.

Her father escorted her to the chapel. At the entrance he stopped for a moment and told his daughter, 'I am so very proud of you.' Then he led her into the chapel and placed her hand into Fellmar's, who was waiting at the altar.

The Bishop performed the ceremony in the time-honoured way. When it came to the vows, only a few people noticed the slight digression from the traditional words for the bride.

'To have and to hold from this day forward, for better for worse, for richer, for poorer, in sickness and in health, to love and to cherish, till death us do part.'

Only the Duke, who had arranged for the missing word, the Duchess and Francine were aware of the deliberate omission of the word 'obey'. Even so, when Francine made her promises, she carefully hid the hand with the crossed fingers in the folds of her gown.

Fellmar had not paid attention to the actual words spoken. It was not until, during the wedding breakfast, that he became aware of the omission when someone twitted him on being very liberal that he did not expect his wife to obey him.

At that point, he became furious since he had expected to use those vows to ensure his wife's compliance. His bride's bland and innocent expression did nothing to reassure him.

Then he changed his mind. He would enjoy bringing her to heel regardless of her lacking vows.

~~MrsB~~

Fellmar wanted to reach his estate before nightfall. That was possible if the newlywed couple left immediately after the wedding breakfast.

Lady Francine's belongings had been sent immediately after the ceremony in a separate carriage. That carriage was the official wedding present from the Duke to his daughter.

Now she and her new husband rode in the Earl's carriage. To her relief, he was surprisingly quiet. The Earl was busy plotting how to ensure his wife's submission. By the time they reached Fell Hall, he had worked out his plan.

~~MrsB~~

On arrival, the Earl and his new wife were greeted by the assembled staff. He introduced her to the senior members, who were happy to have a new mistress.

The Earl instructed his butler to have supper sent to their chambers after they had a chance to refresh themselves.

Then he escorted his bride to the Mistress's suite, which adjoined his own. When they entered her sitting-room, he told Francine, 'If the décor is not to your taste, feel free to change it. These rooms have remained untouched since my previous wife passed away. I thought it best to give you the choice. In this at least,' he smirked. 'I will see you soon.' He left, using the connecting door between their suites.

Francine was to find out that that door could only be locked from his side.

She refreshed herself and washed off the dust from travelling. She was just wondering what to do when her husband entered her sitting-room again. He had not bothered to knock.

'Come, supper has been served.' He extended a hand to her. She took the hand, and he led her to his rooms. The sitting room was richly furnished, with dark woods and red fabrics dominating.

Supper had been laid out on a table by one of the windows. He seated her, then took the seat opposite.

'I presume, since you went through with the ceremony, that you are with child?' he started without a preamble.

'I am,' was her short reply.

'Good. Now here are my rules. They are very simple. You will obey me immediately and in all things.' He raised his hand to stop her from protesting. 'I know you did not promise to obey me when you said your vows. But you will find, it is to your benefit if you do. If you do not, I will punish you, as is my right, as your husband.' He smiled maliciously.

'You will always address me as 'My Lord'. I, of course, will be just as courteous and address you as 'My Lady'. You are, after all, *my* lady. In public, I expect you to be the perfect lady and a credit to my name. Finally, in private, you will serve me in any way I see fit. At any time, I see fit.

Rest assured since you are with child that I will not do anything to endanger my heir. But you will learn that there is much I can do, that will not harm the child, but make you wish that you had obeyed me.

We will spend the next month here, to give you a chance to learn your new role. The walls here are soundproof, so you will not upset the servants with your screams. Although I will take great pleasure in them.

Do we understand each other? My Lady,' he finished tauntingly with a smirk and a raised eyebrow.

'Yes, my lord,' Francine said through gritted teeth. This was worse than she had expected.

Now Fellmar smiled pleasantly. 'Enjoy your supper, my lady. You will need it to keep up your strength.'

~~MrsB~~

The following month made Lady Francine wish she had never been born. Only her innate stubbornness and pride made her survive. But she learned to affect an attitude of nonchalance, even if she did not feel it.

She found that by calmly complying with everything her husband ordered, he became less interested. As long as she could hide the fact of how much she loathed every second of it, she also denied him the pleasure he sought.

It was a subtle revenge on her part, but it was just enough, that he could not break her spirit.

Eventually, he became so bored that he decided that they would relocate to London.

~~MrsB~~

At the beginning of September, Earl and Countess Fellmar made their entrance into London society.

Everyone thought their whirlwind romance and wedding quite romantic. Lady Francine smiled and agreed and was pleasant and charming. In other words, the perfect society wife.

As the weeks went by, the Earl became more frustrated. Since his wife was acting sweet and compliant, no matter what he demanded, his fun had gone out of his marriage. Because he was desperate for an heir, he could not allow the sadistic side of his nature full rein, although he pushed it as far as he dared.

Like tonight. The Earl and his wife were hosting a dinner party. Earlier in the day, Fellmar ensured that Lady Francine was too sore to sit comfortably.

When the guests arrived, she used every possible excuse to move about, rather than sit down. She suffered through dinner, but when the sexes separated after dinner, she enjoyed a short respite, by mostly staying on her feet.

At one point, after the gentlemen had re-joined them, she was about to rise to fetch herself another cup of coffee.

But her husband was being very solicitous 'No my dear, you stay where you are,' he said, pushing down on her shoulder, 'I will get it for you.' He smiled, outwardly the considerate and concerned husband, while inwardly taking pleasure at her discomfort and the fact that she could not protest his attention in public.

He was hoping that he could push her to the point where her composure would crack, and she would humiliate herself, by having to rush from the room in tears. It would be so delightful, to add injury to insult, if he could punish her for her lack of deportment.

His wife's pride and composure foiled him yet again.

He needed to find a new outlet for his interests.

~~MrsB~~

In the months, since his daughter's marriage, the Duke of Denton had been busy with enquiries. He was hampered by the fact that he needed to proceed without raising suspicions amongst his peers. But as a man used to the subtle game of politics, he was well versed in dropping a word here, making a subtle suggestion there. At last, one night at his club, his patience was rewarded. One of his acquaintances started telling his friends about this new courtesan, another friend of his had extolled. She was stunningly beautiful, had exquisite manners, was well-read, but she had exotic tastes in her favours.

'You must have seen her,' he told his friends. 'Braxing is parading Miss Angela Cummings all over town.'

~~MrsB~~

Now that the Duke had not only the name of a potential substitute for his daughter but also the name of someone he knew where to find, he instructed his trusted valet to discover where the *lady* lived.

He had already decided that when he found a suitable woman, he would not contrive an introduction between her and his son-in-law. He would purchase the lady's services and let her arrange to meet the Earl accidentally.

Three days later, his valet had discovered the address and also had the information that the lady would be at home this same afternoon. The Duke changed into a suit which, while obviously expensive, was more discreet than his usual garments.

He presented himself at her establishment which was located in a very modest area. The lady who received him was curious about Mr Smith, who was obviously a man of significant means.

'Mr *Smith*, what an unexpected delight to make your acquaintance,' she emphasised the name with a knowing smirk.

'I am also delighted to meet you, Miss Cummings,' the Duke replied urbanely. 'I have heard much about you, from mutual acquaintances.'

'And you have come to find out for yourself if the stories about me are true?' Miss Cummings seemed amused.

'I have come to find out if you and a friend would suit each other,' Denton corrected gently.

'A friend, is it?' the lady teased. 'Is it not wonderful how many men have such good friends.'

The Duke laughed at the sally. 'In this case, my interest is truly for a friend. My tastes are much less... forceful, shall we say.'

'In that case, what can I do for your friend? He sounds... interesting,' Miss Cummings sounded intrigued and somewhat excited.

'You can let him chase you until you catch him,' the Duke suggested.

She looked surprised. 'He does not know about your visit,' she stated. At his nod, she speculated, 'this friend is not a friend at all, but your son-in-law.'

The Duke raised an eyebrow. 'Intelligent as well as beautiful. He will enjoy that.'

'What makes you think, I will agree to this scheme?' Angela Cummings asked.

'Money,' Denton said pointedly. At Angela's tentative nod, he continued, 'for your exclusive services.'

'That will not be cheap,' the lady explained.

'I never thought you were cheap.' The Duke smiled his most charming smile.

'Very well. Tell me more,' agreed the unsuspecting Earl Fellmar's new mistress.

~~MrsB~~

11 *Life and Death*

1790

Francine Bennet entered the final stages of her confinement. She was relieved that the wait was over. The summer had been very difficult for her in her gravid state. Between the heat and the extra burden which she carried; she was severely out of temper.

But at last, she was going to give birth to the heir of Longbourn. Then her duty as Mr Bennet's wife would be done. Considering the unpleasantness of the marital duties and the effort of carrying the result of those duties, she determined that once was enough.

Now, if only James Bennet would hurry up. He was taking an unconscionably long time to make his way into the world. She had been in labour for nearly thirty hours. She was exhausted from the heat and the now almost constant pain. Her mother was holding her hand and stroking her forehead.

She vaguely heard the midwife, Mrs Jamieson, say, 'Just one more push.' So, she pushed with all her remaining energy. She was rewarded with a feeling of relief. A moment later, she heard the first cry of her son.

She managed a weak smile as, a few minutes later, the midwife put a small, wrapped bundle into her arms and held it to her breast. Her son was beautiful.

Then Mrs Jamieson said with a big smile, 'you have a most beautiful daughter, Mrs Bennet.'

Francine was confused. 'I do not have a daughter. I have a son. The heir to Longbourn.'

'Mrs Bennet, you gave birth to a daughter,' the midwife told her again.

'No, no. I cannot have a daughter. I must have a son. What did you do with my son?' Francine Bennet protested. She could not possibly have gone through all this effort, endured all that she had suffered, for a girl. A daughter. It could not be.

She detached the baby from her breast and held her out to the midwife. 'Take this baby away and give me my son.' Francine sobbed, 'take this impostor away!' She was becoming hysterical. Her mother tried to soothe her.

The midwife, being concerned for the safety of the child, took her from the uncontrollably crying mother. 'I will find a wet-nurse.'

Mrs Gardiner gave the midwife a grateful look before she turned back to her daughter trying to comfort Francine.

On leaving the room, Mrs Jamieson encountered Thomas Bennet rushing up the stairs. He had been alerted to his daughter's arrival by her first cry.

Seeing the midwife with the baby, he broke into a big smile.

The midwife informed him, 'you have a beautiful daughter, Mr Bennet.'

Mr Bennet's face lit up even more. 'A daughter. How wonderful.' His hands reached for the child without a conscious thought.

The midwife was happy to hand the baby to an obviously loving father. Then she explained the problem which had occurred.

Bennet was confused. 'Fanny does not want our child?'

'It appears, since Mrs Bennet expected a son, she cannot grasp the fact that one cannot choose the sex of a child. She was determined to have a son. A daughter is simply not acceptable.'

'But we can have a son in the future.'

'Yes, Mr Bennet, we both know that. But your wife is in no state at the moment to think clearly.'

'Very well, Mrs Jamison. Do you know of a wet-nurse who can look after our daughter?'

'Yes, I do. Mrs Browning had a child last month, but her husband was badly injured in an accident three weeks ago. I am certain that she would be happy to have a position to help in the current situation. Would you speak to Mrs Hill about sending someone for her? I have to return to your wife to help with...' Mrs Jamieson was unsure how much information to give Mr Bennet.

Thomas nodded his thanks to the midwife. 'Please do so. I will speak to Mrs Hill.'

Mr Bennet was relieved that his adorable baby girl would have someone to take care of her even if her mother was unable to do so.

As he descended the stairs Mrs Hill was coming into the Hall. 'Mrs Hill,' he called out. 'Do you know Mrs Browning? We need her as a wet-nurse for my daughter. Please send someone for her.'

Mrs Hill looked somewhat surprised but left to carry out his request.

Thomas Bennet went to his study being completely entranced by the wonderful bundle he gently carried.

~~MrsB~~

Two hours later, Mrs Mary Browning was installed at Longbourn. She had had a bath, a meal, and a new dress, donated by Mrs Emma Bennet.

Mary Browning was a cheerful young woman of five and twenty, who was happy to have the position. This would take pressure off her family, who was taking care of her injured husband.

She had brought her own daughter with her, who was currently sleeping peacefully.

Now Mary was getting acquainted with Miss Bennet under the watchful eye of her grandmother.

'How could anybody not love this little bundle of joy?' Mary asked while the baby was getting her second meal.

Mrs Bennet sighed, 'I suppose, not all women are cut out to be mothers. Poor Francine had a hard time with the birth. I hope she will get over her aberration.'

'Well, Mrs Bennet, I'm very happy to look after this little angel.' Mrs Browning settled happily in her chair, while gently stroking the fine blond hair.

~~MrsB~~

By the same evening, Francine had developed a fever.

She was restless and fretful and kept asking for her James. The fever progressed and nothing which the doctor or the midwife or anyone else could do was helping.

Two days after giving birth to her daughter, Mrs Francine Bennet succumbed to the fever.

Thomas Bennet was sad that his young wife, who only a year ago had been so vibrant, was gone. Although in quiet moments, he admitted to himself that he was relieved that he was no longer tied to someone so vexing. He was ashamed of himself for feeling this way, but he could not help it. A millstone had been lifted from his neck.

Due to the summer heat Mrs Francine Bennet was soon laid to rest. Her husband was the chief mourner at the funeral along with Mr Gardiner and young Edward Gardiner.

This time, Mrs Bennet did not insist on attending the funeral. She stayed at Longbourn in the company of Mrs Gardiner and Miss Martha Gardiner.

A few days later, Jane Bennet was christened. The family had chosen the name for its similarity to James.

The christening was attended by the Gardiner family. Both Martha and Edward fell in love with their little niece.

Mrs Bennet remained at Longbourn as Mistress. Mr Bennet came out of his study to spend time with the two women in his life. His mother and his daughter to whom he was devoted.

~~MrsB~~

In October of the same year, Lady Francine felt the quickening. Assured of the forthcoming arrival of an heir, Fellmar began to make preparations for his future. His will ensured that in case of his own death everything, apart from his wife's jointure, went to his male heir. He also named the Duke of Denton as the guardian of his heir, to provide his son with the best possible entrance to society, should anything happen to himself.

Convinced of his masculinity it never occurred to him that his wife could possibly be carrying a girl. She would not dare.

~~MrsB~~

Only a few days later, Earl Fellmar met Miss Angela Cummings at a party. He was immediately taken by her beauty. She had similar looks to his wife but there the similarity ended.

She flirted with him. Always well within the bounds of propriety but somehow her looks conveyed an invitation. He learned that she was a courtesan and reputedly had exotic tastes.

He was intrigued and used every opportunity to seek her out. She led him a merry chase until, for a considerable remuneration, she agreed to become his mistress.

He purchased a small townhouse in a good location for her. It was far enough away from his own environment that he was not known in the area but still close enough that he could visit easily.

At last, he had found someone who appeared happy to indulge his tastes. He spent as much time as he could in Angela's company, forever bringing trinkets and indulging her expensive whims in return.

Fellmar became so obsessed with Angela Cummings that he almost bankrupted himself. He was barely able to meet his debts of honour.

As the weeks went by, Fellmar had become so preoccupied that he completely ignored his wife, for which Francine was exceedingly grateful.

~~MrsB~~

Ten days before Christmas, Earl Fellmar was again on his way to see his mistress.

Despite the cold weather, he drove his curricle. Being an impatient man, he whipped up his horses and since his attention was on his pleasures to come, he did not pay enough attention to the road. He did not see the rock that was just barely sticking out of the slush which caused his curricle to overturn and ended his libertine ways.

~~MrsB~~

That afternoon Lady Francine received unexpected but very welcome news. While she was in the parlour embroidering a jacket for her baby, the butler, Mr Hastings, entered the room.

Mr Hastings bowed and seemed rather nervous. 'My Lady, I am very much afraid that I have some bad news for you,' he started. 'It appears that the Earl has had an accident. Apparently, his curricle hit a rock which was hidden by the slush. The curricle overturned and Lord Fellmar was thrown out and fell against a wall where he broke his neck,' he finished in a rush, concerned how the young woman would take the news. Ladies in a delicate condition were reputedly easily upset.

'Are you telling me that my husband is dead?' Lady Francine asked quietly.

'Yes, My Lady. I am afraid that is the case.' The butler watched her carefully in case she needed assistance.

'Where is he now? Has someone brought him here, or do we need to send someone to fetch his body?' Lady Francine appeared quite composed.

Mr Hastings started to relax a little. The Countess was not going to go into hysterics as he had feared, after all. 'As luck would have it, the curricle was relatively undamaged. Although the tiger was thrown as well and has a broken arm. And one of the horses is lame. But after the accident, the horses slowed and stopped. Arnold, the tiger, when he found that the Earl had been killed, managed to get some help to right the curricle. Then he had them place the body in the curricle and walked it home.'

'Have you sent for a doctor for Arnold?' Lady Francine was concerned. 'He must be a brave and tough lad to walk here with a broken arm.'

'I was hoping for your permission to send for the doctor.' Mr Hastings was relieved. He liked the boy and wanted that arm fixed properly.

'Looking after Arnold is the first priority. I presume the horses are being taken care of as well?' When Hastings nodded, the widow continued, 'then I suppose you had better get my husband's body cleaned up and laid out decently. Also, take the knocker off the door and prepare the house for mourning. In the meantime, I must write some notes. I expect the Duke and Duchess of Denton will arrive in short order.'

A very relieved butler left the room to carry out his orders. The lady had shown remarkable fortitude.

~~MrsB~~

The Duchess of Denton arrived within the hour.

'I am so sorry, my dear, for your loss,' the Duchess dissimulated. 'I have sent a message to your father. I expect he will be here soon too.'

Lady Francine replied with composure, 'thank you, Mama. It will not be the same without my husband.'

'I expect your life will now be very different. Is there anything I can do for you?'

'I am hoping that you or father will know what arrangements I have to make.'

At that moment the Duke was announced.

'Francine, my dear, I came as soon as I received the news.' He took her hand. 'What can I help you with?'

'I do not know who to contact, to arrange the funeral. I suppose I must also see my husband's solicitor,' Francine replied.

The Duke immediately offered, 'I will be happy to look after all the arrangements for you and speak to the solicitor about the will.'

'Thank you, father. I appreciate your help.'

'In that case, I will leave you with your mother and make all the necessary arrangements.'

As soon as the Duke had left, his wife asked her daughter, 'what are your plans now? Have you thought about it yet?'

Francine gave a slight smile. 'There is something I would like to do, but it depends on your consent.' When the Duchess looked quizzical, Francine explained, 'as soon as everything is settled, I would like to remove to Netherfield. This house and Fell Hall have too many memories of my marriage. And I also do not wish to move back to Denton.'

The Duchess nodded in understanding. 'Yes, I can appreciate your feelings on the matter. Once the funeral is over, I would like you to come to Denton House for a quiet family Christmas. Then in the new year, you can take possession of your estate.' She smiled at her daughter's surprised reaction.

'Netherfield was supposed to be yours, either on your wedding day or your twenty-first birthday. Now seems the opportune time for you to receive your inheritance.'

'Thank you, mother.' Lady Francine was relieved how easily all her problems were now being solved.

Her mother had one more suggestion. 'I am concerned about you being on your own after all that has happened. I truly would feel more comfortable if you invited Anne Hopkins to stay with you for a time. I know she is as much your friend as mine.'

'Will you manage without Anne's help?' Francine was concerned.

'My dear, I have not just lost a husband, and I am also not expecting a child. I am well able to look after myself. And of course, I will be visiting.' The Duchess smiled encouragingly.

'Thank you yet again.'

~~MrsB~~

The Earl was laid to rest with all the ceremony due to a man of his station.

His widow remained composed throughout the service and the reception afterwards which was attended by a surprising number of well-wishers.

Not once did Lady Francine betray her elation at being free from her husband. And if tears of relief threatened, everyone assumed they were tears of grief.

~~MrsB~~

12 *Mistress of Netherfield*

1791

The Duke and Duchess were having a discussion.

If they had been commoners, it would have been called a flaming row. But of course, in their circles nobody would stoop to such a thing. Therefore, they were having a discussion... at the top of their voices.

'Fellmar named me guardian of his heir. Since Francine is carrying said heir, I am her guardian,' the Duke shouted.

'Yes, Denton, I heard you. Fellmar named you the legal guardian of his son. But the child is not yet born; therefore, he does not have a son. If Francine does give birth to a son, you will be the boy's guardian. But until then, you have no right to interfere with Francine. She is not your responsibility anymore. And if the child is a daughter, the daughter will also not be your responsibility since she will not be Fellmar's heir.' The Duchess was frustrated with her husband's attitude.

'But Francine is too young...' the Duke started to protest again.

'She is a widow. She was old enough to get married. She is old enough to be Mistress of a household. She is old enough to be carrying a child. She is certainly old enough to make her own decisions.' Amelia refused to give up and let her husband destroy Francine's life yet again.

'No, Denton. I will not allow Francine to be in a situation again, where another one of your friends could rape my daughter.'

The fight went out of the Duke. 'That was a low blow, madam.'

The Duchess realised what she had said. 'I am sorry. It was cruel of me to say that.' She took a deep breath to calm down. 'Please, let Francine live where she will be happy. Both Denton Manor and Fell Hall are places where she was badly hurt. She suffered months at the hands of that monster. Now she needs time to heal,' she now pleaded.

'Very well, madam. I will wait until the child is born,' the Duke conceded with a sigh.

~~MrsB~~

Within days, Lady Francine was installed at Netherfield Park with Anne Hopkins as company. The Duchess divided her time between Denton Manor to spend time with the twins, and Netherfield, to ensure that Francine was well taken care of.

Lady Francine was grateful. Grateful to be a widow. Grateful to be at Netherfield Park. Grateful that no one could take her new home away from her. And most especially, she was grateful for the company of Anne Hopkins.

After months of abuse, when she had to maintain her composed demeanour, she was exhausted. Now that she could relax, the reality of what she had suffered, caught up with her. One moment, she was elated that her misery was over, the next, she would burst into tears as she relived the horror she had experienced.

At other times, she was angry. Angry at her husband for abusing her. Even angrier at him for enjoying her misery. She was also angry at her father for not protecting her. How could he have been so blind to Fellmar's character?

For weeks, Lady Francine tried to come to terms with her experiences.

Through it all, Anne was there whenever she was needed. Anne did not try to fob her off with platitudes, like telling her everything was fine now.

She listened.

She sympathised. 'I am so very sorry that you had to go through that horror. No matter how hard I try, I cannot imagine the full extent of what you must have felt. No one should have to endure such a marriage. The law and society are incredibly unjust that they do not allow women recourse in such situations.'

She praised. 'You were so strong to deflect your husband. Most women would have broken down. Like, I believe, at least his second wife did. I heard that she killed herself. People believed it was due to her mental state after childbirth. Knowing what we do, I would assume it had more to do with her husband's character. Yet you survived all he could inflict on you.'

Sometimes, she tried to reduce Francine's anger at her father. 'Fellmar was such an accomplished deceiver. There was never any hint of his nature. Even when his previous wives died, no one suspected that he might have been the indirect cause of those deaths. Your father could not have known. On appearances, Fellmar was an excellent match. I know you cannot agree at the moment, but I believe your father had your best interests at heart. After all, he arranged for Miss Angela Cummings to distract your husband.'

That comment eventually roused Francine. 'Who is Miss Angela Cummings?'

'The *lady* your father engaged to distract your husband. The one he spent all his money on. The one he was in such a hurry to see, the day he died.'

'I must find a way to thank the lady,' commented Lady Francine.

After a time, Lady Francine calmed down. Her memories, while still with her, were less immediate. She was slowly starting to heal. But she grieved for the carefree girl she used to be.

~~MrsB~~

During this time, Francine also worried about the child she carried. Would she be able to love it, considering how it was conceived? She thought she would be able to if it was a girl. But if it was a boy, she doubted her ability to forgive.

Rationally, she knew the child was blameless in its father's action. But her feelings could not be regulated by rationality.

In March, the Duchess arrived determined to stay until her grandchild had made its entry into the world and was settled. She prayed it would be a girl.

Three weeks later, just ten days short of nine months since the wedding, Lady Francine went into labour. She was attended by her mother, Anne Hopkins, and Mrs Jamieson, who had been recommended by Mrs Nicholls, the housekeeper.

The fates, possibly to make up for her difficult marriage, granted Lady Francine a quick and easy birth. Within barely two hours, she was delivered of a beautiful daughter.

Never was the birth of a girl so celebrated. Mrs Jamieson, who did not know the history of Lady Francine's marriage, was quite perplexed. Here was a Countess, who was thrilled that her first and only child by the Earl, was a daughter.

Despite the fact that Elizabeth favoured her dark-haired, green-eyed father in looks, Lady Francine immediately fell in love with her precious girl.

It would turn out, that in temperament, she was much closer to her mother – intelligent, witty, and kind. Her impertinence appeared to be entirely her own unless one knew her grandmother intimately.

~~MrsB~~

The day after Elizabeth's birth, the Duke arrived in response to an express sent by the Duchess, to inform him of the birth of his granddaughter.

He went to see his daughter, who was sitting in her bed with the sleeping infant in her arms.

The Dukes usually stern features softened when he beheld the scene before him.

'Good afternoon, Francine. I have heard the good news. You have a beautiful daughter.' He reached out and gently stroked the baby's head.

Elizabeth opened her eyes and reached for the moving hand, accidentally capturing one of the Duke's fingers in her tiny hand. With that move she also captured the Duke's heart.

'Yes, it is excellent news. I am so very happy for you, Francine.' He tore his eyes from the little enchantress to look at his daughter with a broad smile.

'Thank you, father,' replied a perplexed Lady Francine.

'I will inform the new Earl, that his predecessor does not have a male heir; therefore, the title and Fellmar's estate are all his.' The Duke now wore a sarcastic smile. 'I doubt he will be happy with Fellmar's management.'

'I am almost certain that he will not. But he cannot complain to him about it. And he cannot complain to me since I had no hand in my husband's business dealings.' Francine shrugged. 'It and he are irrelevant now.'

After a moment's thought, Lady Francine continued, 'thank you, father, for your help. Please ensure that a certain lady is taken care of.' She smiled the first open smile at her father in a long time.

The Duke looked uncomfortable. 'It was the least I could do, after the mistakes I had made. I am just glad that you have come out of that situation, as well as you appear to have done.'

'But I must let you get some rest. You will need it to look after this little enchantress.' He covered his embarrassment. 'Well, daughter. You are all grown up now and your own woman. I wish you well.'

He gently disengaged his finger from Elizabeth. Then with a nod and a smile at his daughter he left the room.

~~MrsB~~

The following week a letter arrived for The Dowager Countess Fellmar.

London, 19th April, 1791

Lady Francine

I have now taken on my cousin's, your late husband's, title, and estate.

I understand that your jointure was paid out to you, as agreed in your marriage contract which leaves the estate barely solvent.

I am certain that you will understand that as far as the family is concerned, no further contact with you or your daughter will be necessary.

Yours faithfully

Horace, Earl Fellmar

It was beneficial for the new Earl's self-esteem that he was kept in the dark about the response to his letter. It fluctuated between relieved and hysterical laughter.

~~MrsB~~

The Duchess and Lady Francine were discussing Elizabeth's christening. 'I would like to ask Anne to be Elizabeth's godmother.' Francine told her mother.

'My dear girl, I am pleased that you think so highly of Anne. But having her as Elizabeth's godmother would never do. You may not want to move in the first circles, but one day your daughter might. As my granddaughter and the daughter of an Earl, yes even a monstrous one although nobody else knows, she needs a godmother from the first circles.'

Francine tried to protest, but her mother quelled her with a look. 'No, Francine, I will not be denied on this. You may choose to live withdrawn in the country. That is your choice. But do not take the choice away from your daughter. She may have different ideas when she grows up.'

'Very well, mother. I capitulate. I suppose you have someone in mind?'

'Yes, I do. Maria Craven is a charming girl. Very good-natured. I am certain she will be happy to spend a few days in the country, as my guest. I will leave tomorrow to fetch her.'

Ten days later, Elizabeth Anne Fellmar was christened in the church at Meryton, attended by her godmother, Maria Craven, her mother, her maternal grandparents and a friend of the family, Anne Hopkins.

~~MrsB~~

Lady Francine revelled in the fact that she could move again, unencumbered by her daughter. Yes, she loved her daughter, but she preferred her in her crib rather than in her body.

This feeling of lightness contributed to her emotional recovery as well. She could not wait to get out of the house. It was spring, and the weather was getting warmer and more pleasant; she wanted to take pleasure in the fact that she could move again. Although she was technically still in full mourning for another two months, nothing could prevent her now, from acting as the Mistress of the estate.

She had hired a wet-nurse to ease the strain on herself. Now she was getting ready to start visiting the tenants. In the last few months, she had to be content with the steward's reports. Mr Thompson was a fine man and a good steward, but now that she was in residence, she wanted to do her duty which to her was a pleasure.

For the first time in her life, she was in control of her own life. No father to tell her what he expected of her and no husband to placate. The feeling was rather intoxicating.

Now even her mother, whom she loved dearly, was getting ready to leave. Only Anne Hopkins was going to stay at Netherfield Park a little longer. Over the years, she had become much more than a hired companion to both mother and daughter. She had become a friend. Right now, Francine needed that friend more than her mother did; therefore, her mother had decided that Anne should stay.

The ladies stood at the carriage to farewell the Duchess. 'Goodbye, mother. I hope you have a good journey. Give my love to the boys.'

'I will. They still miss their *Aunt Cine*. Maybe the rascals and I will visit sometime? But in the meantime, be well. Enjoy your life and your daughter.' The Duchess smiled and then pulled her daughter into a fierce hug. 'Take care of yourself.'

She released her daughter then let a footman help her into the carriage, where her maid was already waiting. She gave a final wave, as the carriage moved off.

~~MrsB~~

Lady Francine was diligent in her duties as the Mistress of Netherfield Park. Each week she visited the tenants to ensure that there was nothing amiss.

As soon as she was able to ride again, she rode with Mr Thompson to inspect the fields. She went over the account ledgers with the steward and made plans to initiate the crop rotation system, she had read about. She dealt with all manner of business matters.

In the early days, Anne Hopkins was a valuable resource to her. She was able to speak to the servants and gauge their response to their new mistress. On the whole, it was favourable, and when there were issues Lady Francine considered them. In some case, she made changes, in others the servants and the tenants had to learn to adjust.

Yet she still made time to attend to her daughter. She found great pleasure in spending some quiet time holding her child. Admittedly, the nurses were always on hand to deal with the less pleasant aspects of caring for an infant, but she was still considered unusual because she wanted to spend time with the baby.

~~MrsB~~

When her full mourning period was over, Lady Francine very happily changed her black dresses for pale grey. Apart from the hypocrisy of wearing mourning for a man she had loathed, wearing black in the middle of summer would have been unbearable.

It was also time for Anne Hopkins to return to the Duchess.

Lady Francine broached the subject with the lady one morning at breakfast. 'Anne, you know how grateful I am to you for your support these last six months. But I think I am now able to look after myself. And I think my mother misses your company. What are your thoughts on the matter?'

Anne Hopkins smiled, 'I was wondering how soon you would come to this realisation. I am delighted to say that you do not need me any longer.' Then her look turned mischievous. 'I received a letter from the Duchess yesterday, informing me that she would send a carriage for me, two days hence.'

'I am relieved that we all agree on my recovery,' smiled Francine.

Two days later, Anne Hopkins returned to her primary position as companion to the Duchess.

~~MrsB~~

13 New Beginnings

1791

Lady Francine accompanied by a groom rode on her estate. She remembered the first time she rode this way, four years ago. It seemed like a lifetime, so much had happened since.

She wondered how Thomas Bennet was faring. Her sources, in the shape of Anne Hopkins, had informed her that he had married, had a daughter, and was now also widowed. She speculated whether his marriage had been a happy one and whether he was now broken-hearted.

She had often thought about him in the intervening years, particularly in the last one. She had contrasted what she knew about his character with her husband's. Occasionally, late at night, she had fantasised what it might have been like to be married to Thomas Bennet, rather than Fellmar. Although she had found some comfort in these fantasies, they made her reality even more difficult to bear. When she realised that, she had tried very hard not to think about her first and only love.

She was so lost in her thoughts, that she did not realise how far she had ridden when a voice startled her out of her reminiscences.

'Good Morning, Lady Francine,' came the cheerful shout.

Francine reined in her horse and looked at the source of the greeting. There, as if conjured by her mind, was the subject of her musings.

After her momentary surprise, she found her voice. 'Good morning, Mr Bennet.'

'It is a great pleasure to see you again, after all these years. I hope you are well?' Thomas Bennet enquired. Since he was living in a small community, he had heard that Lady Francine had taken up residence at Netherfield Park. But he had not anticipated to meet her so unexpectedly. Now he was struggling to make conversation to prolong the pleasure of seeing her again.

'I am very well now that I live in the country again. I was very sorry to hear that you lost your wife.'

'It is kind of you to say so. Unfortunately, she died of a fever, after the birth of our daughter, Jane. You also have my condolences on the loss of your husband.'

'Thank you. It was very unexpected. He had an unfortunate accident,' Francine replied, although she would always think of it as a very *fortunate* accident.

'My mother and I would have called on you to welcome you to the neighbourhood, but we did not wish to intrude on your grief. Although I understand, you also recently had a joyous event?'

Francine broke into a happy smile when he reminded her of her daughter. 'Yes, I now also have a daughter. Her name is Elizabeth.'

That smile tore a Thomas' heart. He remembered that smile during their previous conversations when they had happily discussed and even argued a point of literature or history. He sternly reminded himself that she had lost her husband only six months ago.

Although his own wife had died less than one year ago, his had not been a happy marriage. Even if he did not miss his wife, that did not mean that she did not miss her husband. He hoped that she had found a love match, even knowing that her father had insisted on a man with the right connections.

But seeing Lady Francine again, made him long for the friendship they had shared. 'Lady Francine, this may be too early, but would you like to have tea with my mother and myself? Any day you are not engaged,' he blurted out.

Lady Francine looked a little surprised but answered with a smile, 'I would happily accept your *mother's* invitation.'

A faint blush crept into Thomas' cheeks that he needed to be reminded of propriety. 'When my mother learns that you are now able to accept callers, I am certain an invitation will be forthcoming presently. I suspect you will receive callers and invitations from all the families in the area.'

'As long as I am not being overwhelmed by visitors or invitations, that would be quite welcome.' Francine smiled. Although she had insisted on propriety, she was thrilled that Thomas Bennet had been so eager to renew their acquaintance as to forget himself.

'But now I must bid you adieu, as I have duties waiting for me.' Francine gave a polite nod and a smile. 'I look forward to seeing your mother again. Please give the lady my regards.'

'I will do so. Goodbye, Lady Francine.'

With a final, 'Goodbye, Mr Bennet,' Francine rode off.

Thomas Bennet stayed at the fence watching her until she was out of sight.

~~MrsB~~

When Thomas Bennet arrived back at Longbourn he entered the house with a spring in his step, which his mother had not observed in nearly two years.

'What has you in such a good mood, Thomas?' she enquired.

'I encountered an old friend on my ride.' He tried to be nonchalant about his meeting.

Mrs Bennet smiled. 'How is Lady Francine?'

Her son looked surprised. 'How did you know, it was her I encountered?' he asked.

'Who else would put such a smile on your face and a spring in your step?' Mrs Bennet laughed. Then she asked more seriously, 'do you still carry a torch for her?'

'You know?' Thomas asked.

Mrs Bennet sighed. 'I have always known. I rightly suspected the Duke would object, so I thought to leave the subject alone. I also thought you chose your wife for her similar looks and name. Am I wrong?'

'No, mother. I expect you are right. I simply never thought too much about it.'

'What will you do now?' Mrs Bennet prompted when her son was lost in thought for a while.

'I am hoping to spend time with her to get to know her again. I believe, four years ago, she returned my feelings. This has probably changed. But I would like to find out. But even if her feelings have changed, I would like her as a friend.' He smiled. 'We used to have some wonderful discussions.'

He finally voiced his request, 'since she is now in half-mourning, it is proper for her to visit with female neighbours. Therefore, would you please invite Lady Francine to tea?'

'I presume you will join us?'

Mr Bennet's only answer was a smile.

~~MrsB~~

Lady Francine arrived for tea, in response to an invitation by Mrs Bennet.

When she was shown into the parlour, Mrs Bennet exclaimed with a smile, 'My dear Lady Francine, it is so good to see you again. Pardon me for saying so, but you now look quite grown up.'

'Mrs Bennet, I am happy to see you too. And I should hope to look grown-up, after all, I have a daughter of my own.' Francine smiled at the warm welcome.

'Please take a seat. Tea will be served presently,' Mrs Bennet invited. 'Thomas may join us later. At the moment we have a small family emergency.'

'Nothing serious, I hope?' Francine was concerned.

'Not too serious, no. Jane is teething again, and it seems that Thomas is the only one who can soothe her at these times. He has been walking around with her for the last five hours. Hopefully, she will settle soon.' Mrs Bennet smiled, half embarrassed and half mischievous.

Francine was incredulous. A man soothing a baby. In her circles that was unheard of. Although, it would probably not be the sort of thing a man would talk about. After all, bringing up children was women's work, and usually those women were the nurses, not the mothers.

She realised she should say something that it was not polite to just sit and stare. Finding her voice, she declared, 'When Mr Bennet spoke of his daughter, he seemed quite taken with her. Although I had not realised, he took such a great interest.'

'Yes, I know my son is quite exceptional.' This time Mrs Bennet was quite proud.

'I hope Mr Bennet is not missing out on tea. Having a young daughter myself, I have no objection to meeting the young lady.' Francine was curious about the toddler who could inspire such affection in a man.

'If you are quite certain that a fretting infant does not trouble you...'

'Quite the contrary. I must admit to great curiosity to meet your granddaughter.' Francine smiled at Mrs Bennet.

'Very well. On your head be it.' Mrs Bennet rang the bell. When Mrs Hill entered, she advised. 'Please tell my son that Lady Francine would like to meet Miss Bennet.'

Mrs Hill withdrew and a minute or so later, Thomas Bennet entered, gently cradling his daughter to his shoulder, and rubbing her back.

'Good afternoon, Lady Francine. I would like to introduce you to my daughter, Jane, but unfortunately, she is in a particularly fretful mood at the moment.' He gave an apologetic smile.

Francine could not resist. She stood up and walked over to where she could see the infant's face. 'She is adorable.' She smiled and without conscious thought, reached out to gently stroke Jane's face.

Jane looked back at her and gave, what sounded like, a happy gurgle. 'Oh please, let me hold her,' Francine begged.

Thomas looked startled, but a glance at Mrs Bennet, who nodded encouragingly, decided him. He carefully handed Jane over.

As soon as the baby rested securely in Lady Francine's arms, she stopped fretting and happily waved her arms about.

Both Thomas and Mrs Bennet looked in amazement at the lovely picture before them.

The moment was interrupted, by a maid who brought in the tea.

'She is a lovely child. I am not surprised that you have quite lost your heart to this little charmer,' said Lady Francine quietly while returning to her seat.

Mr Bennet offered to take Jane again, but Francine with one look at him declined. 'Please, it is no trouble holding her. Let her go to sleep.'

Then she added with a smirk, 'please do not be offended when I say, you look like you could use a break.'

'True. But my mother did not invite you here to play nursemaid to my daughter. She was hoping for some educated feminine conversation.'

'That is quite alright. I can hold a baby and converse at the same time. Are you not aware that most women can do several things simultaneously?'

Mrs Bennet interjected laughingly, 'I have been telling him that for years. Mayhap he will now pay attention since it is coming from you. Now on a serious note. How do you take your tea?'

With that, they settled to enjoy their tea and a pleasant conversation. At some point, Jane fell fast asleep.

~~MrsB~~

As the weeks went by, Mrs Bennet and Thomas were frequent visitors to Netherfield Park.

Both of them insisted on meeting Elizabeth and were immediately charmed by her. To everyone's amazement, Elizabeth reacted to Thomas Bennet, the way Jane had taken to Lady Francine.

While Lady Francine called on her other neighbours and accepted calls from them, her most frequent visits were with the inhabitants of Longbourn.

Sometimes, Francine would encounter Thomas while riding on the estate. They always stopped to chat for a while. They rediscovered each other's interest in literature and had many pleasurable discussions debating the finer points of books they had read.

~~MrsB~~

14 *Healing*

1791

Mr Bennet was shown into the parlour where Lady Francine rose to her feet to greet him with a curtsy. For a change, she had forsaken the grey gowns she customarily wore and had donned a dress in pale lavender. To Thomas Bennet, she looked breathtaking.

Without thinking, he approached and taking her hand bowed and placed a gentle kiss on her bare hand.

Francine snatched back her hand as if it had been burned and hugged her arms to herself.

Thomas was immediately concerned, especially when he noticed her trembling. 'I apologise, Lady Francine, I should not have been so forward. I did not mean to frighten you.'

Shaking her head, Francine swallowed convulsively, then tried to speak. Her words were barely above a whisper. 'You did nothing wrong. Please do not concern yourself.'

'I must have done something for you to be so upset.' When she shook her head again, he persisted, 'you would not react like this if I had not been so inappropriate. I forgot that you are still mourning your husband.'

At those words, Lady Francine could not contain herself any longer, and she spat the words, 'mourn my husband? Mourn the monster who abused me every single day of our marriage?' Her voice rose in anguish, 'after he forced me to marry him? I rejoice in his death!' The last words came out as a shout.

But, as soon as her outburst had run its course her shoulders sagged, and she started to sob. 'But he made me unfit to be anybody's wife again. I cannot bear to be touched by any man since he taught me to expect blows and unspeakable violence.' She turned her back on Thomas.

Thomas tried to soothe her. 'My Lady…'

Before he could get any further, she spun around and snarled, 'do not call me that. Do not *ever* call me those words. *He* used those words whenever he did his worst. He enjoyed adding insult to the injury he caused.'

'I apologise again. I had no idea of what you went through. Please let me help. I care greatly about your wellbeing. I would like to see you happy. I hope that you will at least consider me your friend.' He knew he was babbling, but he had to get them past this anguish.

Normally, he would have tried to use physical contact to soothe her obvious pain, but of course, that was not an option at the moment. Therefore, he had to use words. 'Since I may not use those words as a term of respect, please tell me what I should call my dear friend?' He tried to be as non-threatening as he could, keeping his hands by his side.

At last, his words and posture seemed to have the desired effect. Lady Francine was slowly calming down. 'I apologise most profusely. What must you think of me, to rant like a madwoman?'

'I think you a lady who has been monstrously hurt. Who was not protected as she should have been. Who has been injured by a society, who cruelly blames women for the wrongs of men. I admire you greatly.' Thomas did not have to think about those words; they naturally poured from his lips.

The sincerity of his words was achieving an unexpected but hoped-for result. Lady Francine started to relax, only a trifle to be sure, but it was a start.

'Thank you, Mr Bennet, for your understanding,' she said with a small tremulous smile. 'Please call me Francine when in private. In public, I will have to continue to endure the designation, Lady Francine. But I would like the opportunity to forget it as much as possible.'

'I will be honoured to call you by your given name, Francine. Please do me the favour of calling me Thomas.'

At last, Francine let her arms drop again and she stood up straight. 'I think we could both do with some refreshments. Would you like tea or would you prefer something stronger?

'I think a small brandy to go with the tea, would be a good idea, for both of us.'

~~MrsB~~

Once the tea and the brandy had been served, Francine and Thomas settled into their chairs.

Thomas, after some thought, asked. 'Francine, under the circumstances, can we drop propriety and speak openly?'

'Yes, I think that would be a good idea. I do not want there to be any misunderstandings between us,' Francine agreed.

'Thank you. You see, there are a few things I would like to tell you, which would not normally be discussed even between friends,' he started.

At her nod, he continued, 'some years ago, I met a lovely and intelligent young lady, with whom I fell in love. But her father had other ideas. When she went away, I was heartbroken. Then, two years later, I met another young lady, who reminded me of her. She even had the same given name. Since I could not have the one, I settled for the other.

I had made an enormous mistake. Where one lady had depth, the other was all shiny surface. But I had made my choice, and I was resigned to live with it.

Then, fate intervened. Shortly after Jane was born, my wife died. To my shame, I must admit that I was relieved. Because of that, I can understand your relief at losing your husband. Although my marriage was merely uncomfortable, rather than the horror you went through.

But then I met you again, and the more I discovered and rediscovered about you, I realised that I still love you. If, after your experiences, you can only ever be a friend I will cherish that friendship.'

He then gave a self-deprecating shrug. 'Although I am selfish enough to hope, that given time, you might come to feel the same way I do. Although I pray, you will not feel obliged in any way.'

Francine had listened in growing amazement. This man was so very different from her husband. After all these years, he still measured up to the ideas she had formed at that tender age.

'Thomas, you were not the only one to fall in love that summer,' she started to tell him. 'But, as you said, my father would not allow it. When I came out in society, during my first season, I turned down three offers of marriage because none of them measured up to the scholar I remembered so fondly.' She smiled at the memory.

'Then last year, my choices were taken from me most brutally. It only lasted for a few months, but it left scars.' She laughed a little. 'Since we are being honest rather than proper with each other; I must admit that since coming back to Netherfield and meeting you again, I also realised that I still loved you.

But I am terrified. My head tells me that you are gentle, but my feelings cannot be denied. Now I hate my husband even more. That, by his actions, he may have destroyed all my future happiness as well.'

'Francine, you are a strong woman. I believe that you can overcome anything if you have a mind for it. But rest assured, I will never pressure you and I will always be here for you as a friend.'

Now Thomas smirked just a little. 'You realise that since I have just disqualified myself from ever proposing to you; if you should ever want me as more than just a friend, you will have to take the initiative.'

Francine tilted her head and thought for a moment. 'Then it will be my choice.' She gave Thomas a brilliant smile. 'I like that. Thank you.'

~~MrsB~~

The next few weeks flew by. Both Francine and Thomas were busy with the various chores attendant to the harvest and preparations for the winter.

They often met when riding their estates. Since Mrs Bennet issued a standing invitation for Lady Francine to take tea or dine with the Bennets at any time, they were often in company at Longbourn. Mrs Bennet was often called away due to her claimed duties as Mistress of Longbourn.

Neither Francine nor Thomas believed her, but both were grateful for the subterfuge.

Thomas noticed, but ignored, many half-hearted attempts by Lady Francine to reach out to him and touch his arm or possibly his hand. But she always withdrew her hand again.

Until one afternoon, while laughing at Jane's unsteady attempts to walk, she turned laughingly to Thomas and without thinking took his hand.

It took several moments for either of them to notice the contact since it seemed to be the most natural thing in the world.

When Francine realised what she had done, she looked at their joined hands and said, 'Oh.' After another moment's thought, she released his hand. 'That was not so bad.'

~~MrsB~~

Little by little Francine became used to physical contact which did not cause pain.

She was learning to trust Thomas Bennet, who was doing everything in his power not to rush her or impinge on her personal space.

Whenever he offered his hand to assist her in some way, he always did it in such a manner as to allow her the choice whether to accept or decline.

Francine was fully aware, that even though her mourning period was not technically over, she was being courted in the gentlest fashion. Thomas was keeping his promise to her. He never pushed, or even suggested anything other than friendship. But he was always there.

Someone, with whom she could have a pleasant discussion. Who could cheer her up when she was feeling fretful. A friend, who would listen when the past troubled her.

~~MrsB~~

15 *Changes*

Late 1791

Before they knew it, it was the 16th of December. One year and one day had passed since Earl Fellmar had died.

Lady Francine invited Thomas Bennet to tea. When he arrived, he was amazed to see the lady attired in vibrant blue, matching her eyes.

'You look stunning, Francine.' Thomas could not help but compliment her. 'Has it truly been that long?'

'It has, I am very happy to say. Now I do not have to pretend to be the grieving widow anymore.' She held out her hand to him.

He took the proffered hand and with a questioning look slowly raised it to his lips, giving her enough time to withdraw it if she chose. She did not so choose.

He placed a gentle kiss on her hand which she accepted with a smile.

Tea was then being served and Francine became the perfect hostess preparing his tea just the way he liked it.

'What will you do for Christmas,' asked Thomas.

'I do not yet know. My mother has invited me to spend Christmas with her, but I have no wish to go to Denton.'

'I would like it very much if you and Elizabeth joined us for Christmas,' suggested Thomas.

'That sounds delightful. I cannot remember having a true family Christmas.'

They chatted for a while until Francine seemed to make a decision. 'Thomas, I would like your assistance with something if you would not mind.'

'Certainly, whatever I can do. You know that,' Thomas replied.

Standing up, Francine said, 'thank you.' She walked away from the table. Thomas, being a gentleman, had risen also.

'Could you come here for a minute, please.' Wondering with what she would need help Thomas walked over and stood smiling, in front of her.

'What do you need assistance with?' he asked.

'I would like to try an experiment. Please hold still.' With that instruction, Lady Francine reached up with one hand to cup his face, then stood up on her toes to place a light kiss on his lips.

Thomas Bennet was very glad he had been asked to hold still. He was so stunned that he could not have moved even if he wanted to. Therefore, he stood rock still and enjoyed the sensation of her lips on his.

Francine settled back on her heels and removed her hand with a thoughtful look on her face.

Thomas asked. 'what is the verdict on the outcome of the experiment?'

'It was rather nice. But I think it would be nicer if you cooperated, just a little.'

'Would you like to try again?' was his hopeful question.

Francine smiled. 'Yes, I would.' She again reached up to kiss him and this time he cooperated.

'Much better,' she murmured against his lips.

Eventually, he very gently disengaged himself before telling her. 'My dear, if you keep doing that, you may get more of a reaction that you bargained for. I am not made from stone, after all.' Then he blushed, at the thought of the reaction, her kiss had already caused.

'Then kiss me properly and we will find out if I like it or if I run screaming into the hills.'

He looked searchingly at her face, but only saw a relaxed smile. Hoping for the best, he very carefully took her in his arms and since the smile remained, he proceeded to kiss her *properly*.

When they eventually came up for air, Francine whispered, 'how soon can we be married?'

At that point, Thomas threw caution to the wind and kissed his beloved very improperly.

~~MrsB~~

The following day Thomas Bennet applied for a common licence.

On the following Monday, in the presence of Mrs Bennet and Mr Thompson, Lady Francine married Thomas Bennet and insisted on being known as Mrs Bennet henceforth. Lady Francine was history.

That night, both Mr and Mrs Bennet discovered to their delight, that marital relations could be exceedingly pleasurable for both parties if approached with love, patience, and humour. Further, the respondent sayeth not.

~~MrsB~~

The Duchess, accompanied by Anne Hopkins, was shopping for presents when she encountered an old friend.

'Lord Matlock, how good to see you again,' the Duchess happily greeted him.

'Your Grace, this is a delightful surprise. Are you also shopping for some last-minute Christmas presents?'

'Considering it is still several days till Christmas, it would not be last-minute, as you say. But as a matter of fact, I am buying wedding presents.' The Duchess smiled happily.

'Has your daughter recovered enough, to contemplate marriage again?' Andrew Fitzwilliam was concerned. Over the past year, some rumours about the late Earl Fellmar had started to surface. Since he was dead, no one was interested in pursuing the rumours, but Fitzwilliam tried to stay abreast of anything that was going on.

'It appears she is not contemplating it. She has gone ahead and is already married. I assume it was to present a fait accompli to Denton.'

'In that case, I presume, your husband does not approve of the man she chose.'

'No, he does not. But he will not interfere in her life again. Rest assured, Denton only objects because he is an obscure minor gentleman.

But he is a man of good character, who adores Francine. He does not have a title, but I have known him for years and I approve of the match.'

'When will the announcement be in the paper?' asked Fitzwilliam as curious as ever.

'It will not be in the paper. Francine has chosen to trade Lady Francine for Mrs Bennet.'

'But what about society...'

The duchess turned to Andrew Fitzwilliam, 'please, let society forget about Francine. She is very happy now... in obscurity. She does not need reminders of the past.'

'But what about her children, what about Elizabeth?' was the concerned question.

'Elizabeth will know her parentage and can make her own decisions when the time comes. For now, she will have a chance to grow up in a loving family.'

~~MrsB~~

On Christmas day, while they were in the parlour having tea after a sumptuous Christmas dinner Mrs Emma Bennet addressed her son and daughter-in-law. 'I have come to a decision. In the new year, I will be joining my cousin Susan in Bath.'

'How long will you be staying with her?' asked her son.

'I will go to live with her permanently,' Mrs Bennet clarified.

'Mother Bennet, please do not feel that I wish you gone from your position,' exclaimed Francine. 'I love having your company.'

'It is good of you to say so, my dear, but this decision has nothing to do with you. I had thought of moving when my husband died and only circumstances have kept me here. But now that Longbourn has a proper Mistress and Jane has a loving mother, I am free to leave. This house has too many painful memories for me. Here I lost my husband and my firstborn son.'

She sighed. 'Please do not misunderstand me, I love Thomas as much as I loved Henry, but here I am reminded of my loss every day. Therefore, it is time for me to leave.'

Thomas told his mother, 'we shall miss you. Will you need anything?'

'Susan and I shall do very well together. With both our jointures, we will be quite comfortable indeed.'

'I hope you will visit at least occasionally.'

'We shall see what the future holds,' Mrs Bennet said with a smile.

~~MrsB~~

1792

Early in the new year, the Duke passed away after an evening of over-indulgence. He had had occasional pains in his chest for some months but refused to give in to any weakness until that weakness claimed his life.

The Duchess surprised herself by feeling distraught. When she thought about it, she realised that over the past eighteen months, their worry about Francine had brought them closer than they had been in years, possibly ever.

Her son Alexander stayed sober long enough to make all the arrangements for the funeral and for her continued well-being. He remained at Grover House where he claimed he was comfortably settled.

When the Duchess told him she would now rather stay in town than on the estate by herself, he offered Denton House to her as her permanent home.

He briefly asked after his sister, and when the Duchess informed him that Francine was well, he enquired no further.

His sons had started at Eton the previous fall. Even though he was living in London, which was no great distance from Eton, he had not once made the effort to see them. Instead, the boys had spent Christmas with the Duke and Duchess at Denton Manor.

~~MrsB~~

The Dowager Duchess settled into Denton House.

With the Duke gone, she could now get rid of all those stuffed trophies adorning many of the walls which she had loathed with a passion for the past three decades. The decorations in the house became much more elegant.

When the Easter holidays approached, she collected her grandsons from Eton and installed them in a newly decorated suite, prepared just for them.

Both boys were pleasantly surprised. 'Grandmother, this is not the nursery. Are you certain, you wish us to stay in these rooms?' Alistair asked.

'I am quite certain, Alistair. I felt that as you are becoming young men, you should have rooms suitable to your station.'

Robert was more excited. 'Just wait till we tell the chaps at Eton. They will be green with envy.'

Alistair had more sense. 'That may not be such a good idea, Robert. The older boys will just get jealous and then pick on us.'

Robert was nonchalant. 'Just kick them where it hurts, and they'll leave you alone.'

The Duchess decided it was time to change the subject. 'What would you like to do during your break?'

'The menagerie.' 'The museum.' 'Better yet, riding in Hyde Park.' The boys were getting ever more enthusiastic.

'We shall have to work out a schedule to accommodate all these excursions,' the Duchess laughed. She was going to enjoy the holidays, as much as the boys.

~~MrsB~~

Life settled into a comfortable routine at Longbourn.

Both Mr and Mrs Bennet observed the mourning period for the Duke. Since it was only a few weeks after their wedding, it was a good excuse to focus on each other rather than have to entertain visitors.

Although they did have one regular visitor.

Now that Mrs Bennet resided at Longbourn, Mr Thompson visited regularly, to discuss Netherfield estate matters with the lady. Since Thomas Bennet owned Longbourn, he had no issue with his wife maintaining possession of Netherfield which would pass to Elizabeth at the right time.

Having Mr Thompson visiting to discuss the estate with his wife, had a beneficial side effect for Thomas Bennet. Francine had asked her husband to join these conferences. In the process Thomas learned from the experienced steward, becoming a better master himself.

In addition, since the estates were neighbours, they effectively treated Netherfield and Longbourn as one large estate and coordinated their efforts for the best outcome for both. This made Mr Thompson a very happy man. It also made both estates more profitable.

~~MrsB~~

The other visitor came for social reasons whenever time permitted, and because he was family that did not breach propriety. The surprising aspect of the visitor was that Edward Gardiner came to see his niece every time he came home from Oxford.

Mr Bennet had sponsored his brother-in-law to the university the previous year so that he could have a gentleman's education. He was doing very well, particularly in any subject relating to business.

His sister Martha visited as well on occasion but in her case, it was to visit with Francine, who was only a few years older than herself.

To Martha, Mrs Bennet's manners were a revelation. Like her sister, she had been taught by her mother that she needed to be *lively* to catch a husband. But she did not feel comfortable with those instructions. She had a bubbly personality but the idea of flirting and throwing herself at a man did not sit well with her.

Apart from that, she was developing a friendship with her father's clerk, Mr Paul Phillips. Phillips was exceedingly bright and becoming a very competent solicitor. Since Edward Gardiner showed not the slightest interest in the law, Mr Gardiner was grooming Mr Phillips to be his potential successor.

Now Martha was trying to get a different viewpoint on marriage than the one her mother offered.

'Martha, I have found, the most important aspect of a marriage is that you and your husband should be friends, first and foremost. Yes, Thomas and I love each other, but that love is primarily based on the underlying friendship. If you are lucky, you will find a man who will listen to your opinions.'

'But Mama said that all a girl needs is to be pretty and lively. She should always keep her opinions to herself because men do not want a wife who will argue with them.'

'There is a big difference between discussing opinions and having an argument.'

Martha went home in a thoughtful mood.

Soon, she started to discuss Francine's ideas with her friends, who discussed them with their other friends. Those friends could not resist sharing those thoughts with their mothers as well, and in some cases, even their brothers. Slowly, but surely, a subtle change occurred in the community around Meryton.

~~MrsB~~

16 New Arrivals

1792

Early in the summer, Mrs Bennet confirmed to her husband the good news. She was increasing with their first child.

Thomas Bennet immediately started to fuss. He wanted Francine to take it easy, to rest. He tried to take every little chore from her. Until she could take no more. 'Thomas, stop. I am perfectly healthy. I can manage to walk unassisted. I am not an invalid,' she fumed. 'Please remember, I have done this before. It was no trouble at all.'

Her husband subsided a little. 'I am sorry, my dear. But the only experience I have had was with my first wife. She always needed to rest and found everything exhausting.'

Francine had privately come to the conclusion that his first wife had been a spoiled and lazy child, who always demanded attention. It was not a charitable thought, but she was careful not to voice it.

'I intend no offence to the memory of your wife, but she and I are very different. If I feel I need to rest, you may be certain that I will do so. But even if I need to rest physically, it will not mean that my mind is impaired. I can still sit and discuss estate matters.'

Thomas capitulated, at least on the surface. But that very afternoon he wrote letters, both to his mother and to his mother-in-law, asking for advice. Although secretly he hoped for their support.

He received terse replies from both women, which effectively said, *'Francine is perfectly capable of looking after herself. Stop fussing.'*

He decided that, contrary to popular opinion, women were not the weaker sex.

He still worried, though. Because of that, he paid a great deal of attention to his wife. He realised they had all been correct. While Francine did take afternoon naps most days, she was as active as ever at all other times. To his consternation, but equally to his delight, she also refused to let him neglect his intimate attentions to her.

All in all, Thomas Bennet was a very happy man.

~~MrsB~~

Christmas that year was a very festive time in the Bennet household.

The Dowager Duchess decided, since she wanted to be nearby for Francine's confinement, which was due soon after Christmas, she and her grandsons would spend Christmas at Netherfield. This way, she would be close to her daughter, but the boys would not get underfoot too much.

It also gave Anne Hopkins a chance to spend some time with her family. Most years, the Duchess had spent Christmas at Denton, visiting her family was not a problem for Anne. This year though, the Dowager would be happily occupied with family, allowing Mrs Hopkins several weeks to spend with her now aging parents.

The brothers thoroughly approved of their new uncle, who could tell such wonderful tales. They did not realise that he was actually teaching them history until they were back at school when they learned the dry facts which Uncle Thomas had made sound so exciting.

While the boys and Thomas Bennet were busy, the Dowager had a chance to speak to her daughter.

'You are glowing, Francine,' she told her daughter. 'This marriage certainly becomes you.'

'Being married to a gentle man, who loves me and whom I love, agrees with me. I have never been happier.' Francine could not help but extoll her husband's virtues. 'The most pleasing part is that he believes I have a mind. We have the most wonderful conversations about so many different subjects. Life is never boring.'

'I suppose the girls are also keeping things lively in the household?' her mother smirked.

'Please, mother, do not remind me. Jane is the sweetest, most even-tempered little girl you could ever hope to see. Lizzy, on the other hand, can overset the whole household when she has a mind to. And she is not even two years old yet. The nurse cannot believe that a *girl* could be so curious. She is forever escaping from the nursery and exploring everything. Luckily, she is besotted with Thomas. Lately, we have learned that whenever she goes missing, the first places to look for her are the study and the library.'

'I gather, you find her with him?' The Dowager smiled indulgently.

'Yes, or waiting for him. And he always makes time for her. He could not be a better father to her if she were his natural daughter.' Francine glowed with pride and joy.

'Yes, I can see that, and I am so very happy for you.' The Dowager was relieved and overjoyed that, after the difficult time she had in her first marriage, her daughter was so blessed in her new marriage. Even if the Dowager had not liked Thomas Bennet for himself, for the happiness he instilled in her daughter, she would have adored him.

~~MrsB~~

1793

The day after Twelfth Night, the Dowager relocated to Longbourn, to be on hand when Francine's time came.

The twins went back to Eaton. They felt very grown-up because they were allowed to travel with only a footman for company.

~~MrsB~~

Early one morning in the middle of January, Francine nudged her husband. 'Thomas, please wake up.'

He sleepily opened his eyes and mumbled, 'what is it, dearest?'

'Could you please send for Mrs Jamieson,' his wife requested.

Still not fully awake, he asked, 'who?'

'The midwife,' his wife smirked.

'What!' He sat bolt upright, suddenly wide awake. He hurriedly stumbled out of bed and rushed to the door. 'Hill!' he shouted.

'Put on some clothes,' his wife laughingly admonished him. 'You will scandalise the servants.'

'Let them be scandalised,' he retorted, opening the door, just as he heard footsteps in the corridor. He called, 'send for the midwife.'

He heard the Dowager reinforce his command, 'you heard Mr Bennet. Call the midwife, Hill.'

One set of footsteps retreated quickly down the stairs, whereas another set approached the open door.

In the pale light of dawn, the Dowager, attired in a dressing gown, looked him up and down. 'Very nice, dear boy. I can see what Francine sees in you, but I suggest you had better get dressed. Otherwise, you will scandalise the servants.'

She brushed past him and went to her daughter.

Thomas rolled his eyes, thinking, *What did I do to deserve this?* Nonetheless, he drew on a dressing gown.

~~MrsB~~

Hill returned and reported to Bennet, 'I sent Bob with the trap to fetch Mrs Jamieson. Shall I assist you getting dressed?'

Thomas muttered, 'Et tu brute,' but agreed and led the way to his dressing room.

Once fully attired, he checked on his wife whom he found walking around her room, with the Dowager hovering.

Mr Bennet was immediately concerned. 'Should you be on your feet?'

'Yes, dear, I should,' his wife told him. 'If you are just going to fret, please do it somewhere else.'

Just then, Mrs Hill arrived, leading Mrs Jamieson.

'Good morning, Mrs Bennet. Your Grace.' The midwife greeted the women, then turned to Bennet. 'Good morning, Mr Bennet, may I suggest you get some breakfast, while your wife and I are busy?'

Thomas Bennet knew when he was not wanted and followed her suggestion.

He picked absently at the food Mrs Hill provided for him without actually tasting anything. In the end, he gave up and went to the library to try and take his mind off his wife by trying to read. It was indeed a trying time for him. He smirked at the thought.

Since his first wife had been in labour for more than a day, he wondered how he could occupy his time to stop himself from going crazy.

He heard a cry from upstairs but decided that since it had been but an hour since he had come to the library, it must be Jane or Elizabeth being fretful.

Shortly afterwards, Mrs Hill came into the room. 'Mr Bennet, Mrs Bennet would like to see you,' she announced.

Bennet felt terrified. Men were not welcome during the birthing process. Something must be wrong if his wife wanted to see him at this time. He rushed up the stairs and into his wife's room. The sight he beheld stopped him in his tracks.

There was his wife looking a little tired but very content while holding a baby to her breast. When she noticed his stunned look, a mischievous smile graced her features. 'Would you like to meet your newest daughter?' she asked.

'But how...' he tried to gather his scattered wits.

'It appears that I am made to have babies. I seem to have no trouble at all.' She gave a big smile.

'Thank god for that,' Thomas sighed as he approached the bed. He only had eyes for his beautiful wife and daughter.

'Since it appears, I am just so much furniture, I may as well leave and get some breakfast,' the Dowager smirked. On her way out of the room, she patted Thomas on the arm. 'Congratulations Thomas. She is a lovely girl.'

'They both are,' smiled Thomas Bennet without taking his eyes off his wife.

~~MrsB~~

Soon after the christening of Mary Emma Bennet, her grandmother went back to London leaving the new family to settle into their relationships.

Life became very comfortable for the extended Bennet family. Mr and Mrs Bennet decided that all the girls, irrespective of parentage were *their* children.

'Once she gets older, Elizabeth will have to know about her father and her birthright as a member of the *ton*. She can make her own decisions what she will do about it,' declared Mrs Bennet.

Thomas Bennet agreed with his wife but added with a smile, 'she will always be my beloved daughter, no matter what she chooses.'

~~MrsB~~

The Bennet family spent some very pleasant years, with only minor bursts of excitement.

Late that summer, they were happy to attend the wedding of Miss Martha Gardiner and Mr Paul Phillips. Mr Phillips was invited to move in with the Gardiners since it was decided that he was the logical choice to take over the practice when Mr Gardiner retired. Mr Gardiner suspected that this might not be long in coming since his health was deteriorating.

The following summer Mrs Bennet produced daughter number four for the Bennet family with as little fuss, even from her husband, as previously. Catherine Sophia Bennet was a joy to the whole family, but particularly to four-year-old Jane, who thought her a quite superior doll.

Elizabeth thought the new baby was nice, but not nearly as interesting as her father, who could tell the most wondrous stories.

Mary was still too young to care much about anything other than food, sleep and playing.

~~MrsB~~

The same summer Edward Gardiner finished his studies at Oxford. He came back to Meryton to visit with his family. Because of the shortage of space in his parent's house, Thomas Bennet invited Jane's favourite uncle to spend some time at Longbourn.

In the evenings, they enjoyed having conversations with their after-dinner drinks in the East Parlour, which was pleasantly cool at this time of the year. The windows were open to the breeze, which wafted the scent of flowers into the room.

They were all of a similar age, and because they were not only family but had become good friends, the conversation was very relaxed.

Edward was saying, 'Please do not misunderstand. I knew my sister's faults, but she was still my sister and I loved her. But I am exceedingly grateful that Jane now has you as a role model. It is amazing to see the change you have wrought in Martha. She is still as gregarious as always, but now she tempers her excitement with decorum.'

'Martha is a lovely young woman whose company I enjoy. I was relieved when she, or you, for that matter, did not begrudge my marriage to Thomas.'

'How could I when I saw how lovingly you care for Jane? I hope that one day I will be able to find such a caring wife. But that is still years in the future. Right now, I could not support a family. I need to establish myself first. I was lucky when I was in Oxford that I made quite a few useful contacts. One of them even offered me a partnership when I am ready,' explained Edward.

'What kind of partnership?' asked Thomas.

'Mr Grantley runs an import and export business. He is always looking to expand. He suggested that I should come to work for him, and when I have saved up some money, I could invest it in his business to share in the profits. It seems like a good idea since it would allow me to get to know the business and I could determine whether it would pay me to risk my hard-earned money or not.'

Thomas looked thoughtfully at his wife. She smiled, knowing how his mind worked. She gave a small nod, encouraging him.

'Why not work for Mr Grantley to learn the ins and outs of the business. Then set up in business for yourself?' Thomas suggested.

'I would love to do that, but it will take me years to save enough money to do that,' protested Edward.

'Or find an investor who believes in you,' was the mild answer from Thomas.

'Who would be imprudent enough to invest in an unknown like myself?'

Thomas simply smirked at Edward.

'You cannot be serious,' Edward exclaimed. 'You mean to invest with me?'

'First, I would like you to work for Mr Grantley, or one of your other contacts, for a year. Learn about the business from a practical perspective. In one year, if you can come up with a good plan, we can discuss an investment. After all, in just a few years' time, we will need to provide dowries for four daughters. Therefore, we need to find a way to grow the money we save.'

Early the following year, Thomas Bennet had to revise his estimate. He now had five daughters to provide for.

~~MrsB~~

1796

'Mama, why am I different?' Five-year-old Elizabeth asked her mother. The two of them were sitting on a sofa in the parlour, where Mrs Bennet was showing Elizabeth how to sew.

Mrs Bennet was startled. 'What do you mean my dear?'

'Why do I look different? All my sisters are fair, and I have dark curls.'

'I was going to wait a little longer to tell you about this, but since you ask…' Francine Bennet laid down her sewing and put her arm around her daughter. 'Mr Bennet is my second husband. My first husband was your father. He also had dark hair and green eyes.'

'But what about Jane? She is older than I am, so your first husband must be her father too. But she is blonde.' Elizabeth was puzzled.

'Mr Bennet was also married once before, and Jane is his daughter from that marriage,' Mrs Bennet explained gently. 'Both Jane's mother and your father died. Then, after a while, Mr Bennet and I married and had your other sisters.'

'Does that mean Papa is not my father?' Lizzy was now getting worried.

'Mr Bennet is your Papa in every way that counts. He loves you, cares for you and wants to protect you. That is what a real father does. Just like I also love Jane and you and all your other sisters.'

Lizzy beamed at the idea that had come to her. 'So, it is love that makes us all a family?'

Her mother echoed her smile. 'That is a wonderful definition of a family. Yes, it is that love we all have for each other, that makes us a family.'

Lizzy nodded wisely. 'Good. I like my Papa being my Papa and Jane being my sister.'

Mrs Bennet hid her amused smile. 'I am very happy that you approve.'

~~MrsB~~

17 Family and Friends

1797

Easter was approaching and also Elizabeth's sixth birthday.

Lizzy was exceedingly excited because she had been promised a trip to London, to a shop she had heard had just opened. Unlike most young girls, the shop she was excited about was a bookshop.

To her, having spent much of her life in her father's library, a bookshop was her idea of heaven. So many wonderful stories and facts were contained in those books.

She would also get to spend time with her grandmother, whom she adored.

Since Lizzy had voiced her request for a birthday treat, her parents decided that the whole family should visit London. Francine wished to visit with her mother and Anne Hopkins, whom she had not seen much of in recent years.

When the suggestion for the visit was made to the Dowager, she eagerly approved and insisted that all the children were included in the party.

While Mr Bennet welcomed Lizzy's request for her treat because it gave him the opportunity to improve his library, he had additional motivation to go to London. He wanted to see Edward Gardiner, who had recently set himself up in business, with money invested by Bennet.

According to the reports Gardiner sent, the business was doing well but Bennet wanted to see for himself. He also admitted to himself, that as much as he loved his family, occasionally it was pleasurable to spend time with someone of his own sex.

~~MrsB~~

The Bennet family had been greeted warmly by the Dowager. After the children were taken to a newly refurbished nursery, together with their nurse, Mr and Mrs Bennet were shown to their rooms.

As soon as Elizabeth had refreshed herself, she slipped out of the nursery to stretch her legs in the garden. Although she quite happily sat still to read a book, she also needed to run in the grounds at Longbourn. The Dowager's garden was of course not large enough to run, Lizzy could at least stretch her legs, and there was this wonderful tree which was just perfect for climbing.

Since Lizzy was still dressed in her plainest and most practical dress for travelling, she could not resist the opportunity to clamber around the branches. Eventually, she settled on a comfortable perch on one of the lower branches.

There she was discovered by a pair of boys who were on the brink to be young men. Apart from their dress, they appeared identical.

The one in the fancier ensemble, upon seeing her remarked in a supercilious tone, 'you, girl, what are you doing in that tree. I was not aware that grandmother allowed her servant's children to play in our garden. You had better get back to your mother so that my brother and I can enjoy the fresh air in peace.'

'Leave the girl in peace, Alistair. She is not doing any harm sitting quietly in the tree,' his brother rebuked him.

Elizabeth watched this exchange with amusement but also with a certain amount of ire. 'Who are you to tell me what to do?' she asked, although she suspected, she knew the answer.

The first young man drew himself up proudly. 'I am the Marquess Denmere, grandson to your mother's Mistress,' he declared in a haughty tone.

'My mother does not have a Mistress,' retorted Elizabeth.

'Your father's Mistress then,' Alistair responded indifferently.

'My father is his own master,' Elizabeth played along while suppressing a smirk which threatened to destroy her innocent expression.

Alistair was getting rather annoyed with this little girl who was not in the least deferential to his rank. 'If neither of your parents works for my grandmother, you are obviously trespassing. I have a good mind to thrash you for your offence,' he growled.

'I was taught that gentlemen are supposed to have exquisite manners. As a Marquess, you are assumed to be a gentleman. But threatening young girls is not a gentlemanly thing to do,' replied Elizabeth. After a pause, she pointedly added, 'Cousin.'

Alistair looked affronted. 'How dare you call me cousin. The proper address is Lord Denton,' he exclaimed.

'You are incorrect, *cousin*,' Lizzy emphasised. 'Since you and I share the same grandmother, we are cousins. I am Elizabeth Bennet. I am so very happy to make your acquaintance, cousin,' she added in a saccharine voice and with an insincere smile.

Alistair gaped at his young cousin, while his brother sniggered, then bowed politely to Elizabeth. 'I am your cousin Robert Flinter. I am delighted to meet such a perspicacious family member,' he grinned at Lizzy.

He then turned to Alistair. 'I keep telling you, that those sycophants you like to spend your time with, are turning your head. As our cousin pointed out, as a Marquess, you are supposed to be a gentleman and behave accordingly. Not be so abominably rude to our young cousin.'

'But why did she not introduce herself immediately. I would not have been rude to her,' Alistair tried to defend himself.

'You were rude from the moment you opened your mouth. You immediately assumed she was the daughter of a servant,' Robert retorted.

'But look at how she is dressed...'

'Cousin Alistair, please remember I am present. Do not speak about me as if I was not here,' Elizabeth rebuked. 'You should also consider that for climbing trees, my outfit is much more sensible than a fine dress. After all, I assume you do not wear your best outfit when playing sport.'

Alistair conceded defeat. 'Perhaps I have been somewhat overbearing.' At the sight of the raised eyebrows from both his brother and his cousin, he sighed and amended, 'I apologise for *being* overbearing.' He then faced Elizabeth and asked, 'may I make up for my slight by assisting you down from your seat?'

Elizabeth graciously accepted. 'You may.'

Alistair grasped her by the waist and gently lifted her from her branch and steadied her, while he set her on her feet. 'I truly am sorry I was so rude to you. I was not expecting family in residence.'

Robert interjected, 'Grandmother said, she had a surprise for us. Pray tell, is your father here as well?' he asked of Elizabeth.

'Yes, he is,' replied Lizzy.

Both boys' faces lit up. 'Uncle Thomas is visiting. How wonderful. I must go and find him,' Robert exclaimed. He rushed back into the house.

Alistair gestured toward the house and addressed Elizabeth, 'shall we join him?'

~~MrsB~~

Now that Alistair and Elizabeth were becoming friends, the rest of the visit was very enjoyable for everyone.

When Mr Bennet took Elizabeth to Hatchard's, the brothers accompanied them. This visit was very profitable to the newly established business since three of the four customers were bibliophiles. Even Robert, who was generally more interested in physical pursuits, bought a couple of books on military history. The others spent as much as their budgets would allow. Lizzy even considered her sisters and selected a book of children's stories by Maria Edgeworth for them.

In the end, they needed the help of the footman to carry their purchases to the carriage.

~~MrsB~~

Thomas Bennet accomplished his secondary purpose of the visit to London one rainy day when the family was confined to the house, due to the weather.

His carriage took him the three miles from Denton House to Cheapside, where Gardiner had his warehouse.

Edward was pleased to welcome Thomas and show him around. 'I was lucky,' he explained with a big smile, 'that a few weeks ago, I was able to buy a share of an import, off a man who needed money in a hurry. The ship arrived last week, and I expect to double the money I invested. I expect we will both profit rather handsomely from this venture.'

Bennet was pleased and appropriately complimentary about Gardiner's business acumen. 'If your other ventures perform as well as this one, you will make both of us very rich men.'

'I certainly hope so,' replied Edward, 'but I must admit that I enjoy the excitement that comes with the business.'

'In that case, you are truly a lucky man, Edward. Few men can make a living by doing what they enjoy,' smiled Thomas.

Bennet stayed and watched Gardiner at his work for much of the day until, after delivering an invitation to dine with the family, he went back to Denton House.

~~MrsB~~

1799

Mrs Bennet and her daughters strolled into Meryton to visit with Martha Phillips. The leisurely pace was dictated by the fact that three-year-old Lydia was part of the outing. Despite her short legs she walked along quite sturdily while holding her mother's hand. The other girls were walking in front of the pair.

They were just approaching the Phillips residence when they spotted a distressing sight. A group of boys were tormenting a scruffy-looking dog, who was cowering against a wall.

Five-year-old Kitty, who, of all the sisters was the fondest of animals, could not bear the sight. Without thinking of consequences, she ran across the street, shouting, 'stop it! You are hurting the poor thing!'

Before any of the boys had a chance to react, she had rushed up to the dog and interposed herself between the cowering creature and his tormentors. She faced them with her arms akimbo. 'How would you like it if someone threw stones at you or poked you with sticks?' she demanded. 'You stop it right now and go home.'

The boys were completely nonplussed by this little fury, and they stopped in their tracks. Since she was well dressed, they realised there must be a responsible adult nearby. Looking around, they saw Mrs Bennet approach with a grim look on her face. At that point, they decided that discretion was the better part of valour, and they took to their heels.

As soon as they left Kitty crouched down and gently petted the dog, who licked her hand. 'You poor thing, you must have been terrified. But they are gone now, so you can go home.'

When Kitty stood up to face her mother, so did the dog. 'I am sorry, Mama, that I ran away, but I could not let those boys hurt the poor dog,' she said contritely.

'I am not angry with you,' smiled Mrs Bennet. 'I was angry with the boys. You acted to save the poor creature, which shows you have a good heart. But next time, please think before you act. You might have gotten hurt yourself.'

'I will try, Mama,' promised Kitty.

They re-joined the other girls who were about to enter the Phillips residence.

~~MrsB~~

When the family left Martha Phillips, the dog was waiting for them beside the door.

Mrs Bennet instructed, 'ignore the dog and he will go away.'

She was proven wrong. On the way back to Longbourn, he faithfully limped along beside Kitty. He was aided by the slow pace set by Lydia.

By the time they reached their home, Kitty could bear it no longer. 'Mama, he obviously likes me. May I keep him, please?' she begged.

Only someone with a heart of stone could have resisted the pleading look. Mrs Bennet's heart was softer. 'Very well. You may keep him. But you will look after him. He will be your responsibility entirely,' she agreed.

'Thank you, Mama.' Kitty exclaimed, hugging her mother. Then she crouched to hug the dog. 'I will look after you, and we will be the best of friends. I think I will call you Daniel,' she told the dog with a huge smile.

~~MrsB~~

18 Growing up

1802

'Good afternoon, mother. What an unexpected surprise to see you,' the Duke of Denton greeted the Dowager Duchess.

'I am surprised that you are surprised. After all, I did send a message.'

'Truth to tell, the surprise is not seeing you but seeing you here. Last time you visited, you made it quite clear that you despised my taste... in everything,' he replied, somewhat bitterly.

The Dowager laid a gentle hand on his arm. 'Alexander, you know I had such high expectations for you. I keep hoping you will change your mind and your ways.' She looked at her son, imploringly.

That concerned look made him catch his breath for a moment; then he shook his head. 'No, mother, I cannot take the chance. I would not survive another time. It is better this way.' He moved out of her reach. 'But I do not believe that is the reason for your visit. What can I do for you?'

The Dowager sighed. 'I was desirous for you to host all the family at Denton Manor this Christmas.'

Her son shook his head. 'If you wish to gather the family at Denton Manor then, by all means, go ahead. You know it is your home, and you are free to do as you wish. But I will not join you as I have other plans.' After a moment's thought, he added. 'You can take the opportunity to have a long discussion about crop rotation with the steward; Carter is his name, is it not?'

His mother looked defeated and for a moment the Duke was on the brink of reconsidering his decision. But then he carefully damped down his emotions.

The Dowager was in two minds whether to feel sad or angry. 'You are not the only one in pain. You have hurt Penelope's sons all their lives. I truly wish you would grow up. But I expect it is too late to rescue any potential relationship you might have had with your sons.' Anger won out. She started to take her leave. 'Very well. I will give the family your apologies for your absence, and I will speak to Carter about the crops. I wish you well. Goodbye, Alexander.'

'Goodbye, mother.' The farewell had the sound of finality.

~~MrsB~~

Christmas at Denton Manor was a very festive occasion that year. As planned, the Dowager had asked her daughter and her whole extended family to join her, as well as her grandsons, who were home for the holidays from Cambridge.

The Phillips' had to decline since Mr Gardiner senior had passed away recently. Both Martha and Paul Phillips felt it would be unseemly to attend such a joyous party. In addition, Mrs Gardiner was very much affected by her husband's death. Martha could not in good conscience leave her alone.

The Gardiners were also absent. Edward Gardiner had married Madeline Brooks, the lovely and genteel daughter of a minor gentleman from Lambton, two and a half years prior. Now she was expecting their second child and reluctant to subject herself to the rigours of travel.

Anne Hopkins was present for the first two days of the Bennet's visit which gave her a chance to renew her friendship with Francine Bennet.

The Dowager enjoyed the company of her daughter and granddaughters.

Alistair and Robert were pleased to have Thomas Bennet for company.

~~MrsB~~

One snowy afternoon, the three men were gathered in the library. Alistair, who was still a voracious reader, enjoyed his discussion of books with Thomas Bennet. He liked the different viewpoint Thomas presented which was at such variance from ideas presented by his professors at Cambridge.

Robert, although he liked reading well enough was getting rather bored by the in-depth discussion.

Just then, the door opened, and six-year-old Lydia wandered into the room. 'Hello, Papa, Cousin Alistair, Cousin Robert,' she casually greeted them to announce her presence.

Her father glanced her way and asked, 'why are you not with your sisters, Lydia?'

'They were all discussing *female things*, and I became bored,' Lydia explained. 'I was hoping you would have time for a game of chess, but I guess you are busy too,' she sounded rather disappointed.

Robert saw the forlorn look on Lydia's face. Being kind-hearted and since he was quite fond of all his cousins, he decided that playing a game of chess with a six-year-old was preferable to listening to the others discuss books. Since he was quite good at the game, he thought he might be able to teach Lydia a few things.

Therefore, before her father could respond, Robert told Lydia. 'I admit, I am rather bored with the things your father and my brother are discussing. I would be happy to have a game of chess with you.'

He was rewarded by the brilliant smile that now graced the young girl's countenance. 'Thank you, Cousin Robert. You are now my favourite cousin. Do you want to play in here or shall we go somewhere else?'

Mr Bennet smiled mischievously, 'there is a board set up in the billiard-room. Why not use that one?'

Robert agreed, 'that is a good idea. That way, we will not disturb your discussion with our game.'

'Shall we go and do battle, Cousin Lydia?' Robert invited the girl to come with him.

~~MrsB~~

Lydia and Robert settled at the table in the billiard room, where the chessboard was set up.

Robert asked, 'would you like to go first or second?'

'Second, please,' she responded.

Robert made his first move and then settled to watch his opponent. He was charmed by the look of fierce concentration on Lydia's face.

She responded to his first move.

Robert barely glanced at the board and moved another pawn.

That turned into the pattern for the game. Lydia concentrated on the board to the exclusion of all else.

Robert, on the other hand, watched the girl with amused tolerance and paid very little attention to the game. He had played hundreds of games and playing required little concentration on his part.

That changed when Lydia made a move, then looked up at him with a smile and said, 'checkmate.'

Robert first looked in stunned disbelieve at his young cousin; then he examined the board. To his chagrin, he realised that he had underestimated his young opponent. He truly was in checkmate. There was only one thing to do. He tipped his king over to admit defeat.

'You play very well, indeed,' he complimented his cousin. 'I assume your father taught you?'

'He has taught all of us to play chess. But he is a lot harder to beat than you.' Lydia suddenly clapped her hands over her mouth. 'I am sorry. I think I should not have said that. I did not mean to insult you.'

'I am not insulted. I know your father is an exceptional player,' Robert reassured Lydia.

'He almost always wins,' Lydia declared, proud of her father's abilities. 'Except…' she hesitated, looking uncertain.

Robert became curious. 'Pray tell me what the exception is.'

Lydia now looked embarrassed and fidgeted in her seat. Looking down at her hands, she admitted, 'he says I am a natural at the game.'

'And you beat him?' Robert prompted.

'Not always,' came Lydia's now demure reply.

'What about your other sisters, do they play well?' Robert was curious.

'We have all learned to play, but only Lizzy is good at the game,' explained Lydia.

'I must thank your father for suggesting we play in private. Alistair would be unbearably smug, if he knew I was beaten at my favourite game by a six-year-old. Even worse, since the six-year-old is a *girl*,' he laughed.

'I will not tell him if you do not want me to,' Lydia offered.

Robert thought about it for a moment. 'You can tell him, but only after you have beaten Alistair at the game as well,' he smirked.

Now Lydia laughed as well. 'I would enjoy that,' she admitted.

A few days later, Lydia attained her wish. Alistair's only comment was, 'what is it about six-year-old Bennet girls?'

~~MrsB~~

One evening the Dowager Duchess and her daughter and son-in-law were ensconced in the library in front of the fire. The girls were in their rooms, and the boys had gone to a party at Bridgeview, the neighbouring estate owned by Richard Cartwright.

Mr Bennet was in a thoughtful mood.

'Pray tell, what is on your mind?' his wife asked. 'You seem very distracted tonight.'

'I was thinking about how my life turned out, about how lucky I am to be married to you and I wondered what life would have been like if Fanny had not passed away. I suspect my existence would be very different,' he mused.

'How so?' his wife wondered.

'As I told you years ago, Fanny was a woman of mean understanding and had little interest in anything other than fashion. Before Jane was born, I had started burying myself in my library. I used the pretext that I had to learn about estate management, but I truly just wished to escape her shrill voice and chatter about ribbons and lace. If she had borne five daughters, she would already be frantically considering their marriages and pushing the girls to come out into society as early as possible.'

'I also hate to think what the girls' manners would be like, being raised by a mother who considered beauty the only important attribute in a woman. She would have been horrified at the subjects I am teaching the girls and probably would have opposed any attempt on my part to further their intellect. I am doubtful I would have fought very hard to educate the girls. I might conceivably have been more interested in maintaining my peace.'

'I admit, I also had no real interest in looking after the estate and since it appears that my cousin Collins will inherit Longbourn due to the entail, I perhaps would have become a negligent master. I suspect Fanny would also have overspent her allowance and the girls' dowry would have suffered.'

'Instead, the girls are lovely, intelligent, accomplished and a joy to be around. And thanks to your influence, I have become a more responsible man. The kind of man I can be proud of,' he said with a smile.'

'You have made me a better man, and I am very grateful for that.' He took his wife's hand and kissed it.

~~MrsB~~

19 *Lessons*

1804

Thirteen-year-old Elizabeth knocked on her mother's sitting-room door. The previous day, Mrs Bennet had requested Lizzy's presence for this morning.

Just as her mother opened the door, Mrs Hill arrived with a tea tray. 'That was well-timed, Mrs Hill, thank you. Come in Lizzy and take a seat.'

'I think you may be old enough to deal with some unpleasantness.'

Elizabeth was getting concerned. 'What unpleasantness? Has something happened?'

Her mother gave her a reassuring smile. 'Nothing unpleasant has happened recently or is about to happen. Do not worry.'

Taking a deep breath, Mrs Bennet continued, 'Elizabeth, I need to tell you a story, which is very unpleasant, brutal even, but it has a happy ending.'

Lizzy was ambivalent at this point. She was not certain if she wanted to hear this story, but then she reminded herself of some of the books she had read. Some of them were quite horrific in places. 'Yes, I am ready. What is that story?'

'Once upon a time, there was this young girl, who fell madly in love with a young scholar,' Mrs Bennet began. 'But her father did not approve of the match, so he whisked her away to an ivory tower where he kept her until she was grown up. Then he started to introduce her to men whom he thought suitable for her. He favoured one of them in particular, but his daughter did not like the man. He made her feel very uncomfortable.

Did I mention, this ivory tower was set in rather extensive grounds? Well, it was.

Then one summer, the now grown-up young lady went riding. When she came across this small lake, she stopped to bathe her feet in the cool water. While she was enjoying the refreshing water, she was attacked by the man she did not like.'

Mrs Bennet stopped her tale and looked at Elizabeth searchingly. 'Let us stick to euphemisms for the moment. He took her virtue. Very much against her will.'

Lizzy thought for a moment. 'That is unpleasant to contemplate, but I have read about such things in novels before. Although I wish someone would explain those euphemisms. I always hear that is not appropriate for young ladies. It makes no sense. How can we guard our virtue if we do not know what to guard it from or against?'

Mrs Bennet smiled. It was typical of Elizabeth, wanting to know all the facts. 'Once my story is finished, I will explain everything to you if you still want to know. You may not thank me for giving you this much information.

But to continue my story. Having her virtue taken, the man gloated over the fact that she would now be forced to marry him. Since she was convinced that the act had caused a child to be conceived, and to save her family from ruin, the young woman agreed. They were married soon after. The young woman found out that her husband was as cruel as she had thought him to be, and she was at his mercy, of which he had precious little. But then she had a stroke of luck. Her husband died in an accident, and she was free.

Now we get to the happy part.' Mrs Bennet smiled. 'She moved to the country, where she gave birth to her child. Soon after she encountered her scholar again. They discovered they were still deeply in love. Once her mourning period was over, they married and lived happily ever after.'

'Mama, that was an unpleasant story, but as I said before, it is not much worse than what I have read in novels. What makes it so bad?'

Her mother took her hand. 'The bad part is the identity of the people.' She sighed when Elizabeth gave her a quizzical look. Then she visibly braced herself and continued, 'I was the young woman, you are the child and my first husband, was your father.' Now Elizabeth looked horrified.

She had often wondered about her natural father but her mother's reluctance to speak of that time had prompted her to keep silent. But, as horrific as the truth was, she preferred to know the reasons for her mother's attitudes rather than be forced to speculate.

'How could he? Oh, Mama, I am so sorry. Was it so very bad?' Lizzy threw herself into her mother's arms.

Mrs Bennet gently patted her daughters back. 'Lizzy it was bad at the time but has long been over. And I am very happy now.'

Elizabeth sat up again. 'Oh, I just realised. Papa must be the scholar.' At her mother's nod, she broke into a big smile. 'So, this story has a happy ending indeed.'

'Yes, it does. But I did not tell you this story to make you sad or upset. I wanted to ensure that you understood, this kind of thing can happen to any woman. It can even happen to quite young girls.'

'How can I doubt it, when it happened to my own mother, and I was the result?'

'Now that you know it can happen. I will answer your earlier question. What and how. Are you ready to hear the unvarnished truth about men and women?'

Lizzy swallowed hard and blushed, but her curiosity was stronger than her embarrassment. 'Yes, I do want to know. At least I will know exactly what to guard against.'

'There is one more thing, Lizzy. I also want to teach you how not to be a victim.'

'But Mama, men are usually much bigger and stronger than we are,' Elizabeth protested.

Her mother was regaining her mischievous grin. 'Yes, they are bigger and stronger. But they have some surprising weaknesses.'

Now Mrs Bennet pulled out several books. Mostly they were books on visual art, featuring plates of classical statues and paintings, all featuring the nude male form.

When Lizzy tried to look away after one embarrassed glance, her mother became quite firm with her. 'Lizzy, you know the saying, *know thy enemy*? Unless you look and understand you will never know. Then this morning will have been pointless pain and embarrassment for both of us. Now focus.'

So, Lizzy focused. Even when Mrs Bennet opened the medical texts which she had borrowed from her husband's library. Elizabeth became so engrossed in the technical aspects of what she was learning, she quite forgot her embarrassment.

The final part of her lesson came when Mrs Bennet stood up and discarded the robe she was wearing. Hidden underneath she was wearing a shirt and a pair of her husband's breeches, appropriately padded.

She directed, 'Lizzy, stand up. I will now show you some of the things you can do if a man grabs you against your will and how to take advantage of their weaknesses.'

Mrs Bennet discovered that Elizabeth had inherited a small amount of her father's tendencies. When pushed, she was quite prepared to become utterly vicious.

Under the right or wrong circumstances, depending on one's viewpoint, that could be a very positive attitude.

Mrs Bennet was a happy woman.

~~MrsB~~

Mary Bennet had just finished another disastrous lesson with her music master.

Her sister, Jane, found her sitting at the pianoforte with tears streaming down her face.

Jane, soft-hearted and kind, was immediately concerned. 'Mary, what is wrong? What has you so upset?' She sat down beside her sister and put an arm around her trembling shoulders. At the age of fourteen, Jane took her role as oldest sister exceedingly serious.

When Mary just shook her head, unable to speak, Jane reached into a pocket and extracted a handkerchief which she used to wipe away Mary's tears.

Once Mary calmed down a little under her sister's gentle ministrations, Jane asked again, 'come, Mary, you know you can tell me anything that troubles you.'

'It was my music lesson,' Mary sobbed.

'Was Mrs Trent horrible to you? I am certain we can find you a different teacher...'

'No, not at all,' Mary protested. 'I simply cannot get the music to sound right. I am so careful to get the fingering correct. I pay attention to the timing and the tempo. I even manage to play the various parts, piano or forte, as it is noted on the music. But it still sounds wrong!' she exclaimed in frustration.

Jane listened with concern. Her own playing of the pianoforte was mediocre at best, so she could understand Mary's frustration. But while Jane had trouble even with the fingering, Mary was a competent player. But even Jane had to admit that Mary's playing sounded flat and mechanical. Lizzy, on the other hand, practised less and made mistakes, but she made the music sound alive.

Suddenly, inspiration struck Jane. 'Mary, you know when Lizzy plays the pianoforte, technically she is not as good as you. Do you agree?'

Mary was reluctant to speak ill of her older sister. 'I know she makes a few mistakes in fingering, but she always makes the music sound good. I do not understand it.'

Jane agreed, 'that is exactly my point. Why do you not try to play a piece from memory? Ignore the score. Simply play the music the way you *feel* it should be played. Maybe try one of the pieces that Elizabeth plays well, which you enjoy listening to her play. Then try to convey that feeling.'

Mary looked dubious. 'But what if I make a mistake?'

'That is the point. Do not try to be perfect. Do not play the notes but play the music,' Jane tried to explain.

Her sister reluctantly agreed. 'Very well. I will try.'

After a moment's thought, deciding on the piece of music she could play, she closed her eyes and started to play. She was very hesitant at first, but gradually she grew in confidence until she started to smile and played the music. Not the notes, but the music, just as Jane had advised.

Just as she finished, Mrs Bennet walked into the music room, looking down on the letter she was carrying and said without looking up, 'see

Lizzy; I told you that practising more would improve your playing. That was just beautiful.' Lowering the letter, she looked up and realised that the daughter at the pianoforte was Mary.

'Mary?' she asked in disbelief. 'That was you playing so beautifully?'

When Mary nodded shyly, her mother gave her a huge smile. 'I am so very proud of you, my dear.'

Mary's answering smile could have lit up not just a room, but the whole house.

~~MrsB~~

After Mary had calmed down from her success, she asked her mother, 'Is the letter you have in your hand from grandmother? It looks like her writing.'

Mrs Bennet looked in surprise at the forgotten letter. 'Yes, it is from her. She asks about our plans for the Christmas season. She wondered if we would like to spend it in town, or whether we would like to host her here.'

Jane thought about it for a minute, 'I think I would prefer to spend the holidays here. I was hoping that Uncle Gardiner would bring his family...'

Mary was curious. 'Why is grandmother not spending the holidays at Denton Manor with Alistair and Robert like she usually does?'

Her mother told her, 'Mother says that Alistair has accepted an invitation to spend Christmas with friends. And it appears that Robert has made good his promise and purchased a commission in the Regulars. He was always keen to serve his country and not live off Alistair's charity.'

Mary looked concerned since she rather liked her irrepressible cousin. 'I will pray that he stays safe,' she declared.

'I think we all do,' her mother informed her.

~~MrsB~~

20 Netherfield is let

1805

'Thomas, there is something I would like to discuss with you if you have time,' Mrs Bennet asked her husband after breakfast.

'You know I always have time for you, my dear.' He smiled at her.

'You know, we discussed the possibility of letting out Netherfield since the work of running both estates means you cannot spend as much time with us as you would like,' Mrs Bennet prompted.

'Yes, I remember the discussion. Is there a particular reason why you are raising the subject now?'

'As a matter of fact, I received a letter from Madeline Gardiner. One of Edward's business associates has come into a significant amount of money and would like to see what it would be like to be an estate owner. He is being sensible and has decided to lease an estate, before committing to an outright purchase. Since he still has some business interests, he is looking for an estate fairly close to London. Madeline thought of Netherfield since I mentioned we might consider letting it.'

'Has she told the man about Netherfield or us?' Mr Bennet wanted to know.

'No, she has not. She wanted to make certain that we would be interested, before saying anything,' Mrs Bennet explained.

'I gather since you brought up the subject, you are in favour of the idea.'

'Yes, I am. I am a demanding wife and would like the opportunity to spend more time with my husband.'

Thomas smiled. 'More wives should be as demanding as you.' Then he became serious. 'I have been thinking about this. If we let Edward arrange the lease as our agent, we can keep our names out of the transaction. It would give us a better chance to meet these people as our neighbours, rather than as their landlords.'

'I like your plan. Shall I write to Madeline and have them arrange the lease?'

'Yes, please. And afterwards, your demanding husband would like to spend some time with you,' he teased.

~~MrsB~~

A month later, there was great excitement in Meryton. Netherfield Park had been let. The new tenants had just moved in.

The tenants consisted of a pleasant middle-aged couple, Mr and Mrs Purell, their 15-year-old daughter Beatrice and their slightly older son Peter, who was thought to be about eighteen years of age.

Mr Peter Purell only came for a brief visit at Easter, just after his parents took over the estate, then he went back to Oxford to continue his studies.

Mr Purell spent much of his time with Mr Thompson to learn about estate management. He was very enthusiastic and wanted to know the why and wherefore of every decision Mr Thomson made. Not to interfere or question the steward's decision, Mr Purell simply wanted to learn.

Mrs Purell and Beatrice received visits from all the matrons in the area and then happily returned those calls.

Mr and Mrs Purell even attended one of the assemblies. 'Not to dance, mind you,' as Mrs Purell informed everyone, but to be sociable and get to know their neighbours better.

When his son returned for the summer holidays, Mr Purell tried to involve his son in his lessons in estate management, since the son would inherit the estate, if Mr Purell went ahead with a purchase. Unfortunately, Mr Peter Purell had more of a taste for town rather than the country.

About a fortnight after Peter Purell had arrived at Netherfield, there were some disturbing occurrences amongst the servants, reports of which were passed on to the servants at Longbourn.

Peter Purell was harassing the female servants.

When Mrs Nicholls became aware of the problem, she went to have a word with Mrs Purell, asking her to speak to her son to stop his behaviour.

When that did not produce any results, Mrs Nicholls spoke to Mr Thompson, who passed the information on to Mr Purell.

Nothing seemed to happen for a few more days until one evening Peter Purell accosted yet another maid. This time he did not get a timid little soul, but a young woman with spirit. When he refused to take no for an answer and tried to force the issue, she raked his face with her fingernails and then kneed him where it would hurt the most. Immediately afterwards, she rushed to Mrs Nicholls to complain about the young man.

Before Mrs Nicholls had a chance to discuss the latest breach with either Mr or Mrs Purell, the maid was called by Mr Purell.

'Margaret, what is this I hear about you? You had the audacity to injure my son,' Mr Purell accused.

'Sir, he tried to force his attentions on me. I had no choice,' Margaret protested.

'Of course, you had a choice. All you had to do was lift your skirts and let him have his fun. After all, you are a servant; you are here to serve. If you want to keep your job, you will go to his room now and apologise.' Mr Purell informed the appalled maid.

'You want me to do what?' she exclaimed.

'Go to his room and say you are sorry. Are those words simple enough for you? When he is done with you, you can go back to your regular duties.' Mr Purell was getting rather impatient with the girl. Did they hire half-wits here, since the girl did not seem to understand simple instructions?

'I am sorry, sir, but I will not go to Mr Peter's room. And I will not apologise for defending myself,' Margaret was appalled at the suggestion. 'I was hired as a maid, not a harlot.'

'You were hired to serve. If you refuse to serve, then you are fired. You have a choice, go to his room or leave the house,' Mr Purell coldly stated his ultimatum.

'We will see about that.' Margaret turned on her heel and stormed out of the room. She immediately went to find Mrs Nicholls and explained the latest situation.

Mrs Nicholls was incensed. 'Go and see Mr and Mrs Bennet. They will straighten things out. Do you want me to come with you?'

'That will not be necessary. The Bennets are decent people.' Margaret was relieved to follow Mrs Nicholls' instructions.

She set off at a brisk pace toward Longbourn. When she arrived, she asked Mrs Hill if she could see Mrs Bennet.

Mrs Hill, who had heard about the situation at Netherfield, immediately took her to see her Mistress.

'Excuse me, Mrs Bennet, Margaret would like a word with you.'

Mrs Bennet, who knew all the staff at Netherfield, was instantly concerned. 'Sit down girl and tell me what happened.'

Margaret was only too happy to oblige. She told about the attempts by Peter Purell and then Mr Purell senior's threats.

'Let me see if I understand this correctly. He said he would fire you if you did not give his son exactly what he wants?'

'That is what he said, Mrs Bennet.' Margaret was now starting to have a delayed reaction to the stress she had undergone.

Mrs Bennet reassured the girl. 'You go and let Mrs Hill look after you. Mr Bennet and I will take care of this mess.'

~~MrsB~~

When Francine Bennet reported the problem to her husband, he was incredulous. 'Edward really needs to find better business partners. Who does that man think he is? I will go and see him immediately.'

His wife suggested, 'take the contract.'

With a grim smile, Mr Bennet complied. He had his horse saddled and rode over to Netherfield.

When he arrived, a groom took his horse with a grim smile and the comment, 'very good to see you, sir.'

Mrs Nicholls greeted him at the door and took him to the study. 'Both *gentlemen* are inside.' Her tone gave lie to the word she used. She then knocked on the door and announced Mr Bennet.

Mr Purell senior stood up and greeted his neighbour. 'Ah, Bennet. Good to see you. Do you know my son Peter? Peter, this is Mr Bennet, our neighbour.' Mr Peter Purell stood up and bowed. His face showed very clear marks of Margaret's displeasure.

'Mr Bennet, it is a pleasure to meet you.'

Thomas Bennet acknowledged the introduction with a nod and then commented on the scratch marks. 'You look like you have had an accident.'

Before Peter could say anything, his father interjected, 'the servants in this backwater have no idea about how to behave.'

Thomas pretended concern. 'What do you mean?'

'Would you believe, a maid had the temerity to give him those scratches rather than her favours,' Purell blustered.

'Shocking.'

'I do not know what the world is coming to. Servants are here to serve. If my son wants some girl to serve as his bedwarmer, then that is his right as a gentleman.'

'Are you under the impression that a gentleman can order any servant to his bed whenever it suits him?' Thomas Bennet asked incredulously.

'Of course. Is that not why every man wants to be a gentleman?'

'As a matter of fact, it is not.' Bennet stood up to his full height. 'Gentlemen behave with propriety, decency and honour. They uphold the rights of everyone beholden to them. They do not abuse servants. How would you like it if the local Earl insisted on having his rights with your daughter?'

'But my daughter is the daughter of a gentleman.'

'To an Earl, a gentleman is no higher than a servant is to you.' Bennet raised an eyebrow. 'Therefore, if you think you can do whatever you like with a servant, an Earl would have the same rights with you or your family.'

'But that is not right,' Mr Purell was shocked.

'Exactly. Just as your attitude is not right either. I will not subject the people of this area to a jumped-up tradesman who thinks he is a feudal lord. Or his bratty offspring. Therefore, you will pack up and vacate these premises by the end of the week.'

'Who are you to tell us what to do? I am leasing this estate from Mr Gardiner in London.' Purell was indignant.

'Mr Gardiner is my agent. I am your landlord.'

'Even if you are the landlord, the lease is for a year.'

'You should always read documents you sign, Mr Purell.'

'My solicitor read the lease, and he told me, all of it is above board.'

'It is completely above board. Unfortunately, your solicitor assumed you are a decent man. There is a clause that says that I can cancel the lease if you are abusive to the staff or the tenants. Attempting to rape a maid is abuse. Firing the same maid for not allowing herself to be raped, is also abuse.'

Purell stared at Bennet in horror. 'You are serious about this.'

Bennet nodded. 'Yes. I am very serious. I will also inform Gardiner why I had to cancel your lease. I will now leave you to pack.

Bennet nodded and started to leave the room. In the doorway, he turned back. 'You might like to check the document for yourself. There is another clause you will find interesting. The one that says, you will forfeit any monies paid by you if you break any of the other clauses.'

Just as Bennet was finally leaving, he caught a glimpse of Purell backhanding his son across the scratches and snarling, 'you fool, you have cost me a fortune.'

Bennet winked at Mrs Nicholls as he strode out the front door.

~~MrsB~~

21 Avenging Angel

1809

The Bennet family was visiting with the Dowager in London. The reason for the visit was to present both Jane and Elizabeth at court.

The Dowager had convinced Thomas Bennet that it was in the interest of the girls to do so since it made them more eligible for advantageous marriages.

Mrs Bennet still remembered her time as Lady Francine and was more dubious about the situation.

After much discussion the previous Christmas, when the Dowager had spent a few days at Longbourn, Jane and Elizabeth had agreed to go ahead with the presentation on the principle that it would not hurt.

Now Elizabeth was not so certain. Her grandmother had taken her and Jane to the most fashionable modiste to be fitted for a new wardrobe. Day dresses, walking dresses, evening dresses, ball gowns. Not to mention all the unmentionables.

She was ready to flee back to Longbourn and never see another dressmaker in her life. The only thing that made it bearable for Lizzy was Jane's quiet enthusiasm.

Although Jane was reluctant to admit it, she did enjoy all the lovely fabrics and garments. They had, of course, always been well dressed. Their mother saw to that. But the Dowager's idea of well-dressed was on a totally different level.

But today had been the last fitting. This relatively minor torture was over at last. The major torture continued, practising walking, curtsying, and backing up in a court dress. Those hooped skirts were a torment to move in, for anyone used to the soft flowing styles currently in fashion. But both Jane and Elizabeth were improving. It had been two days since the last time either of them had tripped over the train.

They were on their way back to Denton House, being escorted by Anne Hopkins, as the Dowager's representative, and a trusted footman.

Anne Hopkins smiled at the sisters. 'Your suffering is nearly at its end. Next week you will be presented, and after that, you will have a chance to enjoy yourself.'

'Thank you, Aunt Anne,' said Elizabeth sarcastically to their aunt by courtesy, 'you make me feel so much better.'

Anne laughed. 'You remind me so much of your mother when she was your age. She also had no interest in the fashions and formalities.'

~~MrsB~~

As they returned to Denton House, they discovered that the Dowager had a visitor, despite the fact that polite visiting hours were over.

When the sisters entered the parlour, their grandmother performed the introductions. 'Maria, I would like you to meet my granddaughters, Miss Jane Bennet and Lady Elizabeth Fellmar. Girls, this is Lady Sefton.'

Jane curtsied, while Elizabeth and Lady Sefton politely nodded at each other. Elizabeth was puzzled why her grandmother would introduce her with her father's name.

'Miss Bennet it is a pleasure to meet you at last. I have heard so much about you, that I feel I know you already,' Lady Sefton said to Jane. She then addressed Elizabeth, 'Elizabeth, it has been a very long time since I last saw you. You have grown into an exceedingly lovely young woman.'

Elizabeth was at a loss. This woman addressed her in such a familiar manner, but she had no recollection of ever meeting her. She had, of course, heard of Lady Sefton but was not aware of any relationship between the lady and her own family.

Her grandmother took pity on Lizzy. 'Girls take a seat, and all will be explained,' she smiled.

As soon as Jane and Elizabeth were seated, the Dowager continued. 'Maria did me a great favour about eighteen years ago. She agreed to be godmother to you, Elizabeth; and then kept that fact quiet ever since.'

Elizabeth was startled. 'But why, grandmother?' she asked.

'You needed a godmother from the first circle, but since Francine decided to shun society at every opportunity, I needed someone who would respect my daughter's wishes and privacy. Maria was the perfect choice.' The Dowager smiled fondly at the younger woman.

'Pray tell, why do you acquaint me with this information now?' Elizabeth was trying to get over the shock the disclosure caused her.

'You will need a sponsor for the presentation, Elizabeth. I will be sponsoring Jane, as my protégé; therefore, Maria is the perfect sponsor for you. It also disassociates you from the Bennet name. This will confuse the members of the *ton*.' The renowned mischievous smile graced the features of the Dowager.

'We will divide and conquer,' she laughed. 'Maria and your mother, Lady Francine, will be with you. Thomas and I will be with Jane. This will allow Francine to hide that she is married to Thomas. After the season, she will be able to fade back into obscurity, with none the wiser about who she is now.'

'Grandmother, I now understand from whom Lydia inherited her talent for strategy,' smiled Elizabeth.

She then turned to the smiling Lady Sefton, who had been quietly enjoying her tea, during the conversation. 'I am very happy to make your acquaintance, godmother,' she grinned. 'And I thank you for keeping my mother's secret.'

'It has been my privilege, Elizabeth. Your grandmother has been exceedingly helpful to me over the years as well.'

'Now, we were about to decide, which is the best day for the presentation. Your mother wanted the quietest day we could find, but I disagree. I believe it is best to pick the busiest day. That way, there will be so many young ladies, that two more will go unremarked.'

The Dowager agreed, and the matter was settled.

~~MrsB~~

Lady Elizabeth and Miss Bennet had been presented at court. There had been such a crush of debutants that the two young ladies went completely unnoticed, as planned.

The Dowager and Lady Sefton had arranged invitations to several balls since between them they had connections with everyone who counted in society. In addition, Elizabeth's godmother had provided both sisters with unlimited vouchers to Almack's.

They attended several functions, where Jane's beauty and Elizabeth's title attracted considerable attention.

It did not take long for them to realise that Mrs Bennet had been correct about the quality of the men they met. They were both grateful that they had been warned by their mother that the majority of men would be interested in their connections, their wealth and Elizabeth's title. None seemed to be interested in them as a person.

They decided on attending one final ball, which was the highlight of the current season.

When they arrived, they still maintained the division they had at the presentation. They were greeted by their hosts before they started to mingle.

As the three Ladies strolled toward the refreshment table, they spotted a group of young men in red coats. Lady Francine and Elizabeth were caught by surprise at seeing one particular face in the group. Lady Sefton, the consummate society matron, immediately made the *introductions*.

'Lady Francine, do you remember Major Flinter?'

'Yes, of course, I remember being introduced to the gentleman. Although at the time he was only a Lieutenant.' Turning to Robert, she said, 'congratulations on your promotion, Major. Do you remember my daughter, Lady Elizabeth?'

'It is wonderful to see you again in society, Lady Francine, and of course, I remember Lady Elizabeth. How could I forget so charming a lady?' Robert smiled his most charming smile. 'Might I have the pleasure of the first set with you, Lady Elizabeth? That is of course if I am not too late, and you are already engaged?' he asked as he bowed to Elizabeth.

'You are in luck, Major. We are only just arrived, and you are the first gentleman with whom we have spoken; therefore, I have the set available,' Elizabeth informed her cousin while maintaining her polite smile rather than allowing her impish grin to surface.

'You have made me the happiest of men, Lady Elizabeth,' he responded. He then turned to his fellow officers and declared with a grin, 'I am certain you will excuse me to much more charming company than yourselves.'

The officers naturally agreed, although chagrined that Robert should immediately upon arrival find such congenial company.

Lady Sefton drifted away from the group while Lady Francine led the way to a quiet spot at the side of the room before turning to her nephew. 'Robert, what are you doing in town? I had no idea you would be present.'

'A group of us have just been temporarily posted to the war office. We only arrived today. I had heard from grandmother that you would attend the season and since we received an invitation to this ball, I was hoping to meet you here. I assumed, correctly as it seems, that you would be here rather than at Denton House.'

'I am exceedingly happy to see you. Apart from having you partner Elizabeth; I am pleased to see you apparently well.' Lady Francine turned the last part into a question.

'Yes, I am well. I had a bit of a scrape late last year, but it is all healed up,' he reassured his aunt. 'Are you here alone, or is anyone else from the family present?'

'Mother is here with Jane and her father. I am certain Jane will be happy to have a congenial dance partner if you are so inclined.'

'I will make a point of it. If Jane has grown into the beauty she promised to be when I last saw her, I shall be the envy of all the other officers,' Robert agreed.

~~MrsB~~

Elizabeth and Robert lined up for the first set with the other dancers. They made a rather stunning looking couple. He in his red regimentals and she in a white gown with a subtle pattern of green vines embroidered on all the hems.

They could see Jane across the room in a dress similar to Elizabeth's but with small blue flowers instead of the vines and a few more flowers scattered on the bodice. She also looked exquisite, and her dance partner obviously appreciated her beauty. Elizabeth could tell that Jane thought his admiration was rather too obvious.

'Robert, please make certain you dance the next set with Jane. That man,' she indicated Jane's current partner with a look in his direction, 'is much too familiar for her comfort.'

'I will make a point of dissuading anyone who might have the wrong ideas or intentions,' Robert reassured Lizzy.

For the next set he made good his promise, much to Jane's relief.

'I can now understand mother's attitude to the *ton*. I am only grateful that we have already decided this will be the last ball we attend unless something changes drastically.'

'Seeing all the manoeuvring going on, I am grateful to be a second son,' Robert commented. 'I can attend a ball for the fun of dancing, but nobody has a serious interest in me.'

~~MrsB~~

During a break in the dancing, Jane had moved to a quiet corner to find a seat and rest her feet. She observed another group of young ladies approaching. They did not notice her sitting partly hidden by a pillar.

'Who does she think she is? Have you seen her? She is too short, too brown, and just look at that wild hair. She has nothing to recommend her other than a title. Lady Elizabeth, indeed. I hear she is poor as a church mouse, and yet the men still flock around her. I must wonder why?' the ringleader spitefully denigrated Elizabeth.

Jane, who had listened with growing anger at her beloved sister being so maligned, could not bear to listen any longer.

She stood up and addressed the spokesperson in ringing tones. 'Miss Smith, I realise that as the daughter of a tradesman, you have not had the advantages of a genteel upbringing.'

The young lady so addressed gaped at Jane, who continued her tirade. 'But if you are hoping to move in the first circles it would behove you to learn, to at least *act*, like a lady, even if you can never become a lady. That requires centuries of ingrained knowledge about duty and responsibility.'

Miss Smith tried to interrupt but to no avail. 'True ladies are gracious. They do not act like vicious, gossiping harpies. They have no need to denigrate anyone, to make themselves appear better. They are secure in their position, unlike the social-climbing nobodies with which London ballrooms are now cluttered.'

Jane finished her lecture with a stiff nod, 'now if you will excuse me,' she turned on her heel and stalked away, with her head held high. Inside she was trembling with suppressed anger and astonishment at her outburst, which was a most unusual occurrence for her.

Behind her, there were whispered conversations, since a number of people outside the group she had addressed, had witnessed Jane's harangue. Unfortunately for Miss Smith, her proclivity for vicious gossip was well known. Miss Bennet, on the other hand, had been perceived as a serene angel. Therefore, a number of people had listened with great satisfaction to the dressing down Miss Smith had received. Those same people would now delight in spreading the story of Miss Smith and the *Avenging Angel*.

~~MrsB~~

Two days later, as previously agreed and arranged, the Bennet family removed from town and returned to Longbourn, to the relief of all the ladies.

~~MrsB~~

22 Alexander - RIP at last

1809

A Letter from the Dowager Duchess to Mrs Francine Bennet.

Dear Francine

I hope you and your family are well.

I must share some news which I expect will neither surprise nor shock you. Your brother Alexander passed away last night. He was such a troubled soul while he was alive, yet his passing was strangely peaceful.

It appears he had spent much time sitting outside the other night and caught winter fever.

As his only relation in town, his staff informed me of his illness when it looked like it might be fatal, and I went to see him. It was curious, the more ill he became, the more peaceful he seemed. He was very feverish towards the end and must have been delirious. I was with him when he opened his eyes the last time. He looked at me and smiled and said, 'Penelope you came for me'. He passed away a short time later.

I have arranged to take his body to Denton to have him laid to rest in the family crypt. Alistair will await me there. I felt there was no point in him travelling to London, only to return immediately with his father's remains.

To be frank, considering that Alexander ignored his sons all their lives, I would not expect either Alistair or Robert to be overly concerned with his passing.

The only effect it will have on Alistair is that he will now have the title officially even though he has acted the part of the Master of Denton for many years.

I have just this moment received a note from Robert informing me that he has arrived in town again. He is on leave from the army for the holidays. Maybe he can accompany me to Denton.

Although I disagreed with Alexander's choices and his lifestyle, he was my son, and it grieves me to see him gone so soon. I always hoped that he would come to his senses. Alas, it was not to be. But thinking of last night, I believe all he wanted to do since Penelope died, was to join her. He now has his wish, and at last, he can rest in peace.

Do not trouble yourself by coming to Denton. All will be well. You must stay and look after your own family.

I hope to see you all in London in the new year.

Your loving mother

~~MrsB~~

23 Netherfield is let - again

September 1811

'Francine, my dear,' Mr Bennet addressed his wife at the breakfast table. The mail had been delivered, and he had opened one with a very familiar handwriting. 'It appears Edward has found another tenant for Netherfield.'

'Who does he suggest this time?' his wife asked.

'His latest choice is a Mr Charles Bingley, a young man of about five and twenty years, with a very amiable character and upon enquiry, he is all that he appears to be. He does have two sisters. One of them is married to a Mr Phillip Hurst, the other is unmarried and will be Mr Bingley's hostess. I am afraid Miss Bingley does have a reputation of being difficult to please.'

'Yet another mushroom with delusions of grandeur?' Mrs Bennet enquired with amusement.

'So it appears. What say you? Shall we give them a chance to learn?' Thomas was just as amused. Netherfield seemed to attract a succession of the nouveau riche. But since the leases were always written to ensure that the tenants could do no harm; he had no problem with them wasting their time and money.

The servants had learnt that at the first hint of trouble, the Bennets should be informed, and they would take care of whatever problems arose. They were also well compensated for dealing with novices. Now they were generally just as amused as the owners by the antics of the lessees.

'Why not. As long as Mr Bingley is not vicious, I can see no problem. I wonder which of the servants will win the bet about how long they will last,' Mr Bennet agreed.

~~MrsB~~

A few days later, Mr Bingley presented himself at Longbourn. He had been advised by Edward Gardiner that Mr Bennet, as a favour to the owner, was prepared to show him the estate.

Since all the ladies were visiting with Mrs Phillips, Thomas Bennet was at liberty to show Mr Bingley around.

Charles Bingley was impressed with the manor at Netherfield Park. He was relieved to meet Mr Thompson, who by now had been the steward of the estate for thirty years and was willing to explain the running of the estate to Mr Bingley.

Under the circumstances Bingley was ready to ride back to London, to sign the lease immediately. He expected to move in by Michaelmas.

~~MrsB~~

Word arrived at Longbourn that Mr Bingley had arrived at Netherfield. The rest of the party was expected a few days hence.

To ensure that Bingley settled in with a minimum of excitement, Thomas Bennet rode to Netherfield to welcome the new tenant.

Bingley greeted him amiably and immediately offered refreshments which Bennet happily accepted.

Since the young man seemed perfectly amiable Mr Bennet decided to find out more about him.

'Pardon me for asking,' Bennet started, 'but you seem quite young to be taking on an estate.'

'Not as young as my friend Darcy was when he had to start to run Pemberley. But of course, Pemberley has been in the family for many generations. In my case, it is different. You see, my father was a businessman who made quite a lot of money. When he passed away, he left most of it to me in the hopes that I would purchase an estate and become a true gentleman,' Bingley quite happily explained.

'I was lucky since my father could afford to send me to the best schools. I finished off at Cambridge which is where I met Darcy. He took pity on me when some of the other noble-born students took exception to my attending the same school. He has been helping me ever since.'

'You appear to have been lucky on a number of occasions. Although I must disagree with you about your definition of the best schools.' Bennet smirked. 'Having been to Oxford, I cannot allow you to call Cambridge the best school,' he teased.

'Ah, yes. I have heard this argument on a number of occasions,' Bingley laughed, 'but since I have not been to Oxford, I cannot make a direct comparison. I will grant that you have your opinion and I hope you will grant me mine.'

Bennet was happy to agree to disagree. The rest of the conversation was pleasant and informative for Bingley. He promised to call at Longbourn once he and his sisters had settled in.

~~MrsB~~

Mr Bennet was returning to Longbourn in a good mood. He had enjoyed talking to the young man.

Bingley appeared to be a decent sort. He was polite and he had listened carefully to advice about the estate. There was one bad moment when Bingley commented on the in-depth knowledge Bennet appeared to have about an estate not his own.

Bennet explained his knowledge away as having been neighbours all his life.

Thoughts of his visit distracted Bennet enough that when his horse suddenly spooked, he was unprepared for it.

He had just enough experience and presence of mind to avoid being thrown, but he could not prevent Spirit to collide with an inconveniently placed fencepost. The inconvenience was caused mainly by the fact that his ankle was caught between an irresistible force and an immovable object.

A moment later, he had his horse back under control, but the damage was done. His ankle felt as if it might be broken or at least sprained.

Bennet gritted his teeth and guided Spirit back to Longbourn at a gentle walk to avoid jarring his ankle.

At last, he arrived and called for assistance. He was helped from Spirit and up to his rooms. His wife immediately called for the apothecary to lend his assistance and expertise.

By the time Mr Jones arrived, Bennet's boots had been removed. He felt fortunate when the apothecary diagnosed a bad sprain rather than a break.

Although he would miss the next assembly and dancing with his wife, he would be back on his feet before too long.

~~MrsB~~

24 Full Circle

There was much chatter and laughter in the Bennet household. When five ladies are trying to get ready for a dance, things can get somewhat chaotic.

In due course, Mrs Bennet and the four oldest girls assembled in the parlour dressed in evening wear and their hair becomingly arranged. Their gowns were simply elegant and understated.

'Girls, you all look lovely. You will struggle to sit out any set to give the other ladies a chance. Please be considerate as usual,' she said with a proud smile at all of them.

She turned to her husband and youngest daughter, 'will you two find something with which to amuse yourselves?'

Lydia laughed, 'Papa has accepted my challenge to a game of chess. That should keep us amused.'

'Very well, do not wait up for us. Goodnight my dears.'

With that the ladies entered the waiting carriage to take them to the assembly.

~~MrsB~~

Fitzwilliam Darcy was in a foul mood.

He had come to Meryton to help his friend, Charles Bingley, to establish himself and learn to run an estate.

So now he was at this assembly unwilling to be pleased by anything. He had done his duty by his host and danced one dance each with Bingley's sisters and now he was prowling the edges of the room, scowling.

When Bingley cornered him and pressured him to dance, possibly with the girl sitting nearby, he responded rudely.

'Which do you mean?' and turning around, he looked for a moment in Elizabeth's direction. Turning back to Bingley, and since he wanted his friend to stop pestering him, he said coldly, 'She is tolerable I suppose, but not handsome enough to tempt me. I am in no humour tonight to give consequence to young ladies who are slighted by other men.'

'Don't flatter yourself, sir.' came a voice from behind him...

Mrs Bennet watched with amusement from across the room, as her daughter upbraided the gentleman.

Mr Darcy had some shocks in store for him, in the form of Mrs Bennet's *Surprising* Connections.

~~MrsB~~

Books by Sydney Salier

Unconventional

An Unconventional Education (Book 1) – A P&P Reimagining

Unconventional Ladies (Book 2) – A Regency novel inspired by P&P

The Denton Connection

Don't flatter yourself – A P&P Variation

Mrs Bennet's Surprising Connections – Prequel to 'Don't flatter yourself'

It's a Duke's Life – Sequel to 'Don't flatter yourself'. A P&P spin-off

Lady Alexandra's Hunt – A Regency Romance

P&P Variations

Don't flatter yourself – Revisited – The alternate version of this P&P Variation

Consequence & Consequences – or Ooops – A Regency Romance inspired by P&P

Mr Bennet leaves his study – A Regency Romance based on P&P

No, Mr Darcy – A Regency Romance inspired by P&P

Remember – you wanted this – A collection of P&P variations

Surprise & Serendipity – A P&P Variation

You asked for it – A P&P Variation with a twist

Original Works

Lady Alexandra's Hunt – A Regency Romance

CPSIA information can be obtained
at www.ICGtesting.com
Printed in the USA
LVHW031631080323
741196LV00020B/176